WHAT OTHERS HAVE SAID
WITHIN THESE B

"Stunning. Wow. I'm not sure at this point why your books aren't on the NYTimes Bestseller list...a true talent, my friend. I'm in awe."

—Rachel Thompson, author of *Broken Pieces* and *Broken Places*, on "Hark"

***

"Love this, Justin. Not your typical holiday story. But none of yours are typical, which I love."

—Julie Frayn, author of *Mazie Baby* and *It Isn't Cheating if He's Dead*, on "Hark"

***

"I do so love your holiday short stories. Your voice is crisp and real, and I can depend on you for realism and tragedy, which surrounds many this time of year.

Throughout the read, I knew there would be a turning point, and of course there was the twist, but I must admit I loved the ending—the hope, the possibility even for gratitude... it's not easy at Christmas when everyone pastes a smile and we are forced into a 'happy place' whether we feel it or not.

Bravo, Justin, you captured the feelings perfectly—a sadness and loneliness that many feel during the holidays. It's a passage, a marker of time."

—Eden Baylee, author of *Stranger at Sunset*, on "Hark"

"Loved this story, Justin. Something about it reminded me of how I was after my mom died. I remember that weird surreal feeling when I would wake up from dreaming about her and think that her getting cancer and dying was the dream, and how reality would slowly set in. And that disconnect from other family members especially as time has gone on. Really moving. The ending was perfect. Kudos, my friend."

> —M.E. Franco, author of *Where Will You Run?, Where Will You Hide?*, and *Where Will You Turn? (The Dion Series)*, on "Bracelet"

***

"Great story and loved the ending."

> —Dionne Lister, author of *Shadows of the Realm, A Time of Darkness*, and *Realm of Blood and Fire (The Circle of Talia Trilogy)*, on "Bracelet"

HARK

A Christmas Collection

Justin Bog

Booktrope Editions
Seattle WA 2014

Cover Design by Shari Ryan

Hark—A Christmas Collection is a work of fiction. Names, characters,
places, and incidents either are a part of the author's imagination or are
used fictitiously. Any resemblance to actual persons, living or dead, events,
or locales is entirely coincidental.

Print ISBN 978-1-62015-593-6
EPUB ISBN 978-1-62015-614-8

Library of Congress Control Number: 2014920250

Dedicated to Christopher at Christmastime
and always…

CONTENTS

HARK

WHEN THE TOWN'S TREE LIGHTS UP, I think about the future more than the past. Most of the old timers sitting on the city benches or standing in groups listening to the carolers would tell me to stop living my life worrying over events that are ever unchanging. I'd tell them to stop living their lives with their heads stuck in the sand...bunch of ruminating ostriches.

The tree, in strict accordance with town bylaws, reaches a height of at least twenty feet; it's strung to the gills with white lights (sort of haphazardly placed this year with little symmetry or design). Bo must've been hung over when he threw the lights on, but the others don't complain and don't seem to mind, or are keeping it to themselves, like me. Soon, with gusto, everyone begins to bray out "Hark the Herald," and then the youngest children of the town hang their ornaments on the lower branches, the ones they made in Holy Childhood Day Care—denizens of Whoville. I push the motor-control lever, and my chair buzzes forward an inch or two. The tires are wide and grip like a terror on even the slickest of Michigan's leftover storm ice.

My feet and legs aren't numb, but I think of them as so much frosty cordwood. Colleen, my wife, dresses my lower

half every morning, easy stretch cords and pants, and
my legs weigh nothing at this point, spindly twigs—can't
remember when we last spoke during this morning ritual,
but I do say thank you, or mutter it. Today, she woke up
and asked me if I wanted the wool pants and the extra
warm hunting socks. She knew I'd spend most of my time
downtown, rolling my wheelchair from store to store, as
I usually did, keeping my pleasant demeanor up like a
shield, and end up at Green's for coffee and a honey-wheat
glazed for breakfast, maybe a few poached eggs on multi-
grain toast. Then, I'd wander outside, the motor whirring
and the cushion of my seat hardening in the cold (I can't
feel the chill. I have to lift myself off the chair hourly for
a minute, if I can, so I don't develop sores—my version
of planking—and my upper body strength is a marvel. I
was always the kid the beach bully kicked sand at until I
enrolled in the police officer training program—a buddy
there taught me how to lift weights, and I grew confident
as the lifting changed my appearance, bulked it up). I'd take
my usual position next to the corner real estate office and
watch the cars go by and say hello to the business people
walking past, brisk with errands on the mind, wrapped legs,
meandering down the street to open their shops. And I only
watch their legs move away from me and think of myself. I
notice dozens of averted gazes each morning, and it doesn't
bother me anymore; who wants to stare at my shriveled up
legs anymore. I don't even want to.

   I meet Colleen at Mary Ellen's, Gurney's for take-out
sandwiches if the weather's not too salty, or Turkey's for
lunch during the winter months because a few of the other
restaurants are closed for the season, operating under lim-
ited hours, or too gosh-darn expensive. Besides, since I'm
a regular I get the easy banter from the waitresses and the
cordial treatment, no pauses or glances from strangers who
wonder how I lost movement in my legs and lower spine.

Afterwards, Colleen and I head home, where I can help her cut vegetables or whatever she needs to make dinner. I've always done my share, and we've learned to get past my handicap and form a bond. I've only seen her cry once over me, and I let her cry, didn't scold her at all. I didn't even push the door to our bedroom in and try to hold her. I let her cry everything right out of her like weak smoke.

She's sitting next to me on the bench and I take her gloved hand in mine and press gently. Colleen sings the next song, *The First Noel*, with a seasoned voice, full from years in the church choir, and she returns my touch with a squeeze of her own.

* * *

I was a townie police officer five years ago—the anniversary of this singular moment, something I don't mark on the calendar hanging at chair height next to the dishwasher. I'd worked on the force for fifteen years when the call came on the radio. I had dreams, too. I loved this town. Harbor Springs hid its advantages right alongside unspoken-of disadvantages. Very little riff raff, a couple icy accidents on the curvy road heading towards Good Hart, few burglaries, and seldom do we report to a murder scene.

The call from the station came in cryptic and coded, told me someone on the Point reported the snap of a low-powered rifle. There were only three families living out in the Harbor Point Association during offseason. The Point is a peninsula of land that shoots out into the water and forms a secluded bay for the town, forms the picturesque post cards embracing yesteryear nostalgia. It's private property with old cottages lining both sides. The wealthier people come up during the summer months and open their homes. These people keep the money flowing through the area businesses, and the local people have always had bones of contention to pick with them about who really has roots in the city and who just uses their services, even though the city would dry up like a prune if Harbor Point burned to the ground.

When I pulled into the gate and checked Earl Shadd's, the security guard's, cabin, I found it empty and a note written on his log sheet: *Checking Dodgeson cottage 11:15 p.m.* And I forgot to spell out it was Christmas Eve because it adds to my story–I try to be clear. No one should've been out on the point. I knew the Dodgeson clan was at the town tree-lighting ceremony, Merchant's night, and they attended every other town Christmas celebration, so I knew their late dinner at The Pier turned into Midnight Mass over at the church. They were a family I never thought twice about. Their routine during the holiday was a given until now. I drove out to their cottage, unwariness pinging away and changing into an intuitive buzzing annoyance. Earl's security car was parked out front along with a blue van I didn't recognize. When I got out of my car I noticed the heavy tracking of footprints in the snow, from house to van and back again over and over. I unsnapped my holster, dropped back to my car and radioed for backup, which would be the state cruiser on the way to Petoskey. As quiet as a Christmas mouse—I actually remember having this thought—I made my way up the front walk, and was there halfway between house and cruiser, when a man dressed in black came out of the house carrying wrapped packages and a crystal lamp. He dropped everything, the glass shattering on the porch, the presents skittering down the icy steps, and ran back into the house. I yelled at him to stop and come out with his hands up and was very surprised when he did just that not a minute later. He wore a black ski mask, black gloves, jacket, pants, and shoes. The only parts of his body showing were his eyes and the pale red of his lips. I told him to come down the steps and motioned with my gun, pointed towards my squad car, and, when I retrace this night in my mind, I always come back to the footprints in the snow, so many of them, and the almost fatal mistake I made by disregarding the information in front of me. So many of them I curse myself and wonder why I acted the way I did because the other man dressed like the first ran around the back of the house and came up behind me. I heard the gunfire at the same time I felt the fiery pain in my back. The next thing I knew I was lying face flat on the ground, and I couldn't feel anything. I heard their van engine start and the sound of them pulling away, as I cursed my own stupidity, crying because I'd never been shot before, not up here in Harbor Springs, a town so postcard perfect I knew my own story would be shoved under the carpet in due time, and with the utmost respect.

*   *   *

Colleen pulls the blanket surrounding my body tighter against my waist and I thank her. She never asked me what happened and I don't think she ever will. All I know is that she's mine and always will be. The people of the town form a circle around the tree and begin to move to the left. I watch them and their legs dressed in winter wool and bright colors, moving so freely, and I think about that Christmas five years ago when my spine shattered and the long rehabilitation in Northern Michigan Hospital, when Christmas was taken away from me, and I can't help my own bitterness, how I tend to it.

*   *   *

One of the men in the van lived with his family outside of Cross Village on State Road, in a trailer. The other man was his brother, up from down state, penniless—among a growing Michigan horde of desperate citizens—I cannot blame him...I do not blame him...I'm reconciled—and trying to get a job at the local ski hill for the winter as a groomer. It was a simple matter really. They were poor and wanted to provide something good for The Wife and the two bewildered children on the holiday. And it really is a matter of economics and how people are pushed inside until they burst. But they killed Earl Shadd (he at least made it inside the Harbor Point house, startled and confronted the thieves, and paid too high a price) and made my life a living hell, and I won't let this town forget about it because I'm here every single day sitting in my chair, the motorized one the police department bought and presented to me when I got out of the hospital months later, after tests and operations to remove bone splinters, after grueling weeks of physical therapy. The Wife came to visit one afternoon with my brow dripping sweat from the exercises my physical therapist made me do every other day. Colleen had vanished down to the cafeteria, and this woman came in and introduced herself and told me how sorry she was. I screamed at her to get out. I pushed myself up so far I almost fell off the bed and I screamed at her some more as her features twitched and she backed out of the room. The nurse ran in and helped me regain my balance. I turned my head away so she wouldn't see me if I started crying. I've done my share of that and I swore I'd never cry again. Policemen don't cry. You seldom see them do it though, and I know, believe me, they do.

*   *   *

It's late when we return home. Colleen removes her coat, and I can't help being myself. I want to be alone. Colleen pulls my knit cap off and kisses the top of my head. She understands.

There's nothing I can do on Christmas Eve, but I want to love, and I want to forgive, and I want so much my mind splinters the way any mind does when thoughts rush forward in manic patterns—replaying choices, currying regrets. Christmas will arrive and Colleen will drive us over to her brother's house in Charlevoix. He and his wife teach in the school system, political science and government for Jared, and American history for Patti. Colleen and I never chose to have kids. That's what we tell ourselves.

We'll have turkey, bacon-wrapped and roasting the day away, cornbread stuffing made with sausage and mushrooms, my favorite, and then we'll try to laugh at the state of Jared's football picks, debate politics with their two college-age kids, and, after the kids leave for parties, they'll talk about their expenses, how frugal they have to be. Patti will once again pull Colleen aside and ask how she's holding up…

I'm always dreaming of driving over to the Point, replaying the scene, and sometimes in these dreams I do become aware of the second thief and still end up facedown in the snow, spine shattered, the pain, ghostly, waking me up in a sweat. These dreams are fading. Nowadays, I dream of singing, Christmas carols, the town belting out holiday cheer, and I listen…I listen to every note…*Peace on earth and mercy mild…God and sinners reconciled.*

The End

SEDUCING SANTA

IT'S CHRISTMAS EVE and I have the whole night planned. I make dark chocolate rum cookies and spread them artistically on my good French china and, afterwards, I take a bath with jasmine-scented skin softener. I put on a new red lacy negligee, with a matching (warmer if I'm going to wait long) robe with dainty, feathery slippers, the kind that look like you have racy pompoms on your feet. I light all the candles in my living room—tall ones, thin ones, and wide ones, placed on the bookshelves and the end tables, and turn off all the house illumination except for the flickering white lights of my small, tabletop Christmas tree. Then, I settle a bottle of Veuve Clicquot Rosé into the ice bucket, ready to serve, and sit on my puffy couch, my legs tucked under me, waiting.

* * *

Is it silly to want someone so badly you'd do anything to be around that person? I'm known as a person who doesn't rein in her passions. The Mr. Spocks of this world can kiss my sweet personality. Believe me, I'm really not speaking as any kind of stalker. I've never been a fan of celebrity. And, no, I didn't have a poster of Kurt Cobain or Luke Perry on my wall …really (Okay—I will say one thing—I don't think Courtney Love is a great role model. Who does she think she is anyway?). I'm not that desperate. You be the judge. Ask me if it's silly to want someone so badly you'd act like a complete fool, I'd have to answer: no, with reservations, of course. I think murder is out of the question. I can't think of any situation where I'd kill someone just to get what I want. On the other hand, I've been thinking about Mrs. Claus a lot.

I picture the goody goody the day after Christmas, rocking in her chair because she can't help being in motion even while sitting—she worries about her husband too much. As a kid, whenever Christmas rolled around and a teacher, parent, art mentor, said, "Draw Santa and Mrs. Claus," ten to one, everyone sketched Mrs. Claus in a red dress (the more talented would make it gingham), a bonnet to match, tiny wire-rim glasses, rocking away in some wooden rocker, knitting her husband a new red suit for next year's jaunt. But I wouldn't kill Mrs. Claus; I couldn't. And I'm just fantasizing anyway. Who I really want is the jolly St. Nick himself, the world's chimneysweeper and master reindeer-whipper.

I have a very cool personality, aloof if you will. I find it hard to choose men because I never want long, binding relationships. I don't think it's possible for one person to love another person so much that they mate for life. For true love to happen you need to have separation, a little distance to make yourself realize that love can rub you raw. I couldn't be with someone else every hour of every day anyway. Look at Romeo and Juliet. When they were running around, meeting secretly, kissing each other passionately, they had the most fun. It's only when they started to contemplate being together forever that problems and poisoning occurred.

*   *   *

I run my own candle-making business in the upscale town of Petoskey, where it's sometimes hard to make a living, and in this economic climate, nearly impossible for the less established businesses. The townies support the locals who've been here forever, and my family has been here since the town was incorporated. I never left after high school. Northern Michigan is not the place to be to start a business you think will thrive all year long. It just won't happen, but the tourist trade from late spring to Labor Day and a few weekends after that keeps me solvent. Electrical storms are also welcome in my book; if the power goes out, people buy more of my candles. Anyway, I'm one realistic woman who doesn't expect the glittery extravagances surrounding her to make her world glow with happiness. And, I repeat to myself—it's like a daily, sickening new-age mantra—this: I don't really need a man to make me happy. (Why need a man when I can have a mantra daily?) Up here in northern Michigan the pickings are slim to none if you're into men, and I am into men every once in awhile, but like I said, I'm very aloof and a bit choosy. If I date, on average, more than one man in a twelve-month period I call it a banner year. Running my own business keeps me too busy to take on a stray.

*   *   *

Three years ago, when I first opened Wick and Wax, I met a man named Rudy at the Mitchell Street Pub. He was sitting at the bar watching World Wrestling Entertainment. Later, even though I knew the answer to my own question and was just playing the slightly confused shorthaired brunette, a defensive role, I asked Rudy what WWE stood for. Then, I, dimly cringing inside, asked Rudy why it was changed from WWF—the F for Federation somehow made more sense to me, although, currently, I didn't follow any sports. Who has the time? With my newly found retail knowledge I knew that most athletes didn't buy candles in large quantities. I studied Rudy as he sipped a foreign beer out of a fancy bottle. I sat at a table close by and surveyed the crowd: a Wednesday night with maybe fifteen others who sat huddled in the booths, couples with wine, party drinks and loud laughter. Rudy intrigued…

He had this big red nose. I mean, in an animal fable, I would've said: it almost glowed. I didn't know if he had low self-esteem problems like most of the vagabonds who escaped to this part of the state. If he was teased as a kid a lot, I didn't want to mention his nose since I thought it made him unique…intriguing. I'm no spring beauty queen either. I don't have any real wishes, maybe a little more on the bust and, perhaps, a bit hacked away from the back of my thighs, yet I do yearn to wake up one morning so wickedly gorgeous I'd have twenty reputable men pounding at my door. That night at the Pub, however, you got what you got. Rudy was a catch; he was the only man who sat alone without a wedding band, and this is important to me because I think married men expect too much, and I've never fallen for any member of that tribe, never ever ever ever have I ever been interested in a married man before. They're like bullies on a school playground, rings forefront and still pestering all the girls, all at once, the worst of them leading Betty behind the slide and telling her she's the only one, when in fact, little Cindy Lou or Noelle would also suit his needs, hiding his wedding band in his inner suit pocket, the kind with the button. I want a man who wants one thing only, and that's me. I took my drink, scotch and water, and sat next to Rudy.

Even after a lifetime subscription to Cosmopolitan, I didn't know how to start a flirtatious conversation. I didn't want to be seen as forward by asking him if he was, in fact, married and happy with three kids back home in Charlevoix where he worked, if he worked, and when he smiled and said, "Yes," have to slink away, and not in a good way. Boring small talk makes me wince. I asked Rudy if he knew a lot about wrestling and told him a distant cousin was on the pro circuit. Rudy looked at me, and said, "Oh yeah?"

"Yes," I improvised, "His stage name is the Phantom of the Mat. He wears one of those half-white Phantom faces and a black cape lined with red silk. Have you ever seen him wrestle?"

Rudy looked me in the face, his red nose barely half a foot away from mine, and said, "Lady, my name's Rudy, but I don't know anyone named the Phantom of the Mat." Then he started laughing, and I almost left right then, I mean, why wouldn't he believe an honest, sincere woman who comes up to him at a bar. Was I that obvious? His jolly laughter held me there.

I replied, nervous, and in motor-mouth mode, "My name's Laura, and I just opened my own candle store here in Petoskey four months ago." I did stand up to leave then, but he grasped my hand and said, "It's nice to meet you, Laura."

Okay. We went back to his apartment and he told me all about his nose and how growing up was humiliating because his brothers wouldn't let him play with them and made such fun of him, ostracizing him at an early age. Now he couldn't care less. I said his nose was sexy. He told me he liked the way I made up stories. I told him I'd give him a call the following week, but I never did. I see him around town from time to time. I mean, I always recognize his nose first and scurry away in the opposite direction.

* * *

A couple months after that my coworker, Sandy, set me up on a blind date with a cousin of hers from Cheboygan. His name was Elton, which struck me as kind of unusual and curious. As long as he was a single man and as long as he wasn't a dud, I could date an Elton. Somehow his name struck me as a bit snobbish, British, and I know that's a stereotype, but Elton John is British, so put two and two together. I make connections.

Anyway, Elton met me halfway between Cheboygan and Petoskey at the Douglas Lake Bar, which serves wonderful Steak au Poivre. He said he'd be wearing a red shirt. Once again, I grew more captivated. How did he know red was my favorite color? Sandy must've told him. My candles come in twenty different shades of red, all the way down to soft bubblegum pink. The rose candles are perennial best sellers.

Okay, so I walked into the restaurant and I saw Elton. Instant attraction. He had a short-whiskered white beard and he looked like he was about ten years older than me, and I'm only in my early thirties, honest. His hands were clasped around his belly, and it was the first thing I noticed. I knew this night had possibilities. We made small talk over an appetizer of Shrimp Louie, and I couldn't take my eyes off his red shirt and his large gut. He wasn't plump anywhere else—he had muscular forearms—but his belly, it was round like a basketball, and it jiggled on its own when he laughed at my silly observations about the other, much older, Harbor Point, upper-crust diners—this is where the moneyed crowd goes to hide from those who lost it all, pretend that the country wasn't sinking into quicksand.

Elton also had these twinkling green eyes. They exuded good cheer and fun times, and I wanted to reach out and stroke the fine white hairs of his beard, but I restrained myself. He told me he was a plant manager for Procter & Gamble, and that he might be out of a job if the plant shut down, which was a rumor then. I don't know where he is now, probably down state, at a different plant; I didn't keep in touch with him after he took me home, which was a-okay with me.

One night and I had my fill. I needed to distance myself again, work up to my next lover. Elton was really sweet and all but, like I said, I need to love someone from far away. Sandy asked me all about the date and I told her it was wonderful and meant it. She smiled and said she was so happy for me, but I didn't give her any details; they were personal, just between Elton and me. He had the softest, rosiest skin, and he made love like a slow, smooth burner, a circle of blue flame. Sandy quit the next year thinking me too cold, too businesslike, and didn't understand why I wouldn't return her cousin's phone calls.

*   *   *

It's been much more than a year since Elton, and my fantasy life has taken over. Here I lay, spread out on my couch, waiting. The ice in the champagne bucket melted an hour ago and it's now the middle of the night. The cookies sit untouched and I can just make out the scent of rum. I wanted St. Nick to be knocked out by them, a little tipsy and warm, some willing flesh on a cold Christmas night. After Elton, I got a reputation. Men weren't interested in me anymore. Sandy and Rudy must've talked to a lot of people about me, given me a reputation as a "love 'em and leave 'em" kind of woman. I get surface chatter from the locals, small talk. I cringe whenever I pass someone who says hello to me on the street for fear they'll stop me and talk about the weather. But I do get lonely. I pined for Rudy and Elton, my few physical encounters, but I wouldn't act on my feelings; if I had, the memories would break, the beautiful fire I kept inside, unlit, those two nights of splendor, would be ripped away, torn into bitter fragments of longing.

My plan formed the closer Christmas came. I asked myself: Who is the one man who has all the physical and mental aspects that I love? Who is the only man who could keep a secret? Who would know if I was naughty or nice? It became obvious, and I went out of my mind trying to find someone who would clean my chimney on such short notice. I even shoveled the snow off my roof and pointed my outdoor lights up at the sky to make landing easier.

But it's now almost two o'clock in the morning, and I don't know if I just woke up from a dream or if I never went to sleep because Santa is standing across the room from me in front of my fireplace, shaking a finger at me as if to tell me, "No peeking, little one. You should be in bed." He has a face full of white whiskers, and his red suit is almost black with chimney soot, but not from my chimney; I cleaned mine.

I rub my eyes and think about the men in my life and realize he, the truest love, comes every year. All I had to do was be good. Santa unbuckles his belt, wordlessly, and lets it drop to the floor. He flings off his black boots and his red bellbottoms, leaving his silky boxer shorts. I can't believe my eyes when he shrugs off his fur-lined coat. His belly is enormous and jolly, and he rubs around his belly button. I glance at his nose and compare it to Rudy's. Santa's is more defined but redder as if he'd spent the last two months having it shined and pampered by a hundred spa elves. When my eyes meet his, they sparkle like sunlight across melting glaciers.

He walks toward me, his cheeks becoming rosier with each passing second. Then he kneels down in front of me. He looks up at me and says, "Have you been good all year?" His voice is steady and strong and I tell him, "You know everything. That's why you're here. You know what I want."

He kisses my hand and rises up to kiss my lips, scratching whiskers against my softened skin. This is what I've been waiting for. This is the end of my dreams—my body is now in tune, a tightened wire—the one true love who will leave and not feel cheated, the man who will come back every year to fulfill a bond and not fret over the separation. He'll hold me in his heart, his memories, all year long, and have one more incentive to get out of the house on December 25th and do his duty—the kind of gift that keeps on giving.

Then, right when he plants the kiss on my parted lips, Mrs. Claus's image hammers into my thoughts. She's angry, her lips form a slashing frown, and snarling sounds come from her throat. She flings her bonnet to the floor. Her white curls cascade around her shoulders, and I swear I see the hair grow longer. Her wire-rim glasses fly across the small elf-built living room somewhere near the North Pole. I don't know if what I'm seeing is real or not, but I push Santa away and scoot out from underneath him.

"What's wrong, my little candy cane?" Santa sinks back to his knees and his eyes plead with me.

"What will your wife think?" I say this like any soap-opera star ready to jilt a previously accepted lover.

Santa stands and holds out his left hand to show me his ring finger, which has no gold wedding band. I'm about to ask him if he's hiding his vow ring inside his red jacket's buttoned pocket. My question is stopped short when Mrs. Claus's image reappears, shoving itself into my mind, she's there, terribly distraught, flying out of her house and across the arctic snow field, freezing, elves chasing her, as she runs from what is about to happen half a world away in the small Michigan home of a lonely woman, and I realize there can be true love in this world, and not the kind of true love I had always defined by chilly emotional distance. The kind of love that is unconditional. Wake up. Find it. Live it. I hear this new mantra in my head and wonder if this is his present to me.

Santa sits next to me on the couch, but this time he just holds my hand and the images seep in. He's with his wife, outside their house, kneeling in the snow, arm in arm, and telling her she's the only one, and he'll never break her trust even if he has to come close to show people that love can form bonds that last forever. Two people, together all the days of the year, except one, and they are happy. I want to ask St. Nick about the charade, his undressing in my living room if only to get a merry laugh out of him, but I keep the impulse at bay.

I kiss St. Nick on the cheek and hand him his pants and say, "Thank you."

With a rejuvenated twinkle in his eyes he tells me I've received the greatest gift tonight, and I want to believe him. He disappears up the chimney and the last I hear is a raucous "Ho, HO, HOOOOO," and the crack of a whip.

When I wake up Christmas morning all alone I still want to believe him.

The End

BRACELET

CALLIE LOST THE BRACELET. It's all she can think about: how she could be so absentminded. Christmas is right around the corner and Callie misplaced Maggie's, her sister's, present. She can't sleep well at night because her actions keep repeating in her mind, trying to find a clue to where the gift will be found. It's eating a wiry pit in her stomach.

Last April, Callie stopped in an antique store up the Puget Sound's Chuckanut coastline in the town of Fairhaven, shuffled around a bit, sifted through shelves of odds and ends, and spotted the bracelet where it sparkled on green velvet under hazy glass—an almost eerie match to her mother's ring (Callie was immediately drawn to the bracelet and knew she'd buy it within seconds of finding it), which she had sent Maggie two years before. While Maggie had three kids, Callie didn't have any children of her own to pass the jewelry to because of her accident long ago.

The antique gold bracelet needed polishing. It incorporated the same design as the ring: three carved diamonds in delicate La Belle Epoch finery, with one larger diamond inset where the band widened. It cost Callie enough to make her worry about her savings, the looming recession, the school levy, and the next fundraiser for the community swimming pool—Callie loved to swim and do water aerobics three mornings a week at the Fidalgo Island Pool, laugh with her friends Carmel, who worked behind the desk checking swimmers in, Harriet, and Mary Lou—they could always lift her spirits. The water also soothed, being the only place her injuries didn't matter, where she felt buoyant in body and mind.

Her parents, both firm disciplinarians, raised Callie and Maggie, in utmost fashion, to always be giving people; they, with an almost zealous stridency, emphasized what other people would like or what others needed before filling their own empty bowls. Callie bought the perfect, matching bracelet on the same impulse—it was needed—and put it out of her mind. She drove back to Anacortes, her home on the first island in the San Juan Islands chain, where her husband, John, had bought the small white, green-shuttered house on 8th Street and J Avenue, near the public library and close to Causland Park. John had been a career military man, and he was stationed at the base on Whidbey Island. By the time Callie washed her hair, prepared an art project for her students, and read a chapter of the latest P.D. James on the kindle Maggie gifted to her the previous birthday, the bracelet was already lost.

Callie teaches art at the island's high school, but she doesn't have seniority. The elementary art teacher, Mr. Wright, has been there longer. In the emergency vote, if the levy doesn't pass, Callie will be suspended after the spring term and out of work within a year, right along with ten other teachers and programs. She has money enough in her savings to last for a long time, money from her husband's insurance policy filled it up and left Callie feeling even more alone at home. She told Maggie she'd give the money back in a flash if John would only return, healthy. She knew if she had to stay home every hour of every day, she'd realize her loss even more. In part, Callie teaches the children to give her a purpose, and the delight on their faces when they create something out of the simplest tools mends her unhappiness.

Losing her job was a rumor back in April when she bought Maggie the bracelet. Now, December 20th, it's a reality. The first levy vote fell, and Callie's on notice of suspension until they re-vote in February. She thinks about only teaching until June, only having six more months in her classroom, about never firing the irritable kiln again, never sending the roughest children to the principal's office for throwing clay or paint at each other; she dreams about saying goodbye to the other teachers, trying to find some other job, striving to stay cheery even though she knows she's too old to compete in the area's job market. Visions of going to Colorado to stay with her sister flit to the surface from time to time, and she forces them back— and the image of her setting up shop next to her father in Surprise, Arizona, digs into her mindset as well. Callie stocks up on antacids.

There's no way she could leave the peace of The Sound, all the wild birds that migrate to her feeders in the spring, the Arts Festival in the summer, the scary-fun Halloween party at the town marina, all of her friends who visit often, and her dearest pals who share her love of films at the Anacortes Cinema and a bottle of wine at The Brown Lantern pub afterwards to dissect Hollywood's offerings—the easy laughter of friends as close as family to Callie; there's no way she could leave John, whose ashes fell into the cold water between Fidalgo and Lopez Island. Sometimes she sits on a bench in Washington Park for an hour at a time watching the ferry boat travel to the outlying islands, stopping at Lopez Island first, long and visible from her bench—a place to walk and find hidden beauty in the yesteryear pace. John took Callie there once every summer, and they'd picnic on Reuben sandwiches and pickles from

Gere a Deli at Watmough Bay, a pristine hidden beach
where yachts anchored and other visitors were scarce.

* * *

The December chill of morning wakes Callie up and she's
glad school's over for the year. All the teachers whose jobs
are secure scurry away from any future dread, giving Callie
forced cheer: "You'll see, Cal. People love you here." But
Callie's next thought is always that all the love in the world
won't save jobs. Where she left the sparkling bracelet nags
inside her. She can't believe she'd ever misplace anything,
let alone her sister's Christmas present, anything with so
much meaning and value.

Callie has slept off and on and dreamt of a sketchy wan-
dering about town, a following of her regular path among
the birches down to the boat docks, up past the tennis courts
where, in the summer, young children are taught to swing
forehands and serve by a gruff coach—his hectoring always
making Callie grin since she knows well how children often
stray from any planned lesson. In her dream, she's arm in arm
with John, who steadies her walk; somehow right beside her,
even though he died five years before, bone cancer withering
him away to splinters while Callie waited, covering him up so
she couldn't see him beneath the white t-shirts he wore. She
forced herself to stay by his side and thought, "How many
quilts will it take to bring him to peace, softly, with no pain?"

After untangling the covers from around her feet Callie
doesn't remember her dream and the happiness of her
walk under the trees. The images flicker out and become
overshadowed once more by, "It's almost Christmas and
the bracelet. Where is it?" She mutters, "John? If you were
here you'd tell me. I know you would. You'd remember."

Callie hunts through her trunk at the end of her bed and
brings her mother's old holiday quilt out, red and green

overlapping circles, intricate and warm. She wraps herself in it, grasps her cane and moves out of her bedroom. After noticing the drift of snow, she decides to call Ben Ditty in an hour to shovel her walkway. It rarely snows in Anacortes so close to the water, but this year the first, and perhaps only, snowfall, blanketed her neighborhood, the cookie-cutter Victorian homes disappearing in the whiteness.

Soon, Callie sets coffee bubbling and a slice of raisin bread toasting. In the back of her mind different locations to search in the house pop in and out of memory. Did she put the bracelet in the top drawer of her dresser? In the box of wrapping paper? Did she leave it in her old purse, the one she threw away last summer? How can she find it in time to send it to Maggie? And her sister takes over her thoughts. Maggie, ten years younger, settled more than half the country away in Colorado, with a living husband, and their three children, Sheila, Mark, and George, the oldest, the one with the old family name, their father's namesake. Maggie didn't grow up with Callie because Callie moved away when Maggie was still a young child and only moved back to the farm for her last two years of high school, where the energy in the home made Callie feel like she sat on the largest cushions of pins and needles. People thought Callie would never walk again after a tractor rolled over her on the family farm — her father a corn and cattle farmer, staying the course for the past three generations, until her parents went sonless. They sold in their senior years — her mother passing on almost eight years ago now, and her father living in a retirement community in Surprise, Arizona, his health worries a constant undercurrent whenever Callie speaks to him or her sister.

When she was but a child, her teenage years right around the corner, the accident caused Callie's pelvic area to fracture and a complicated network of internal damage weakened her system for almost a year — she would never have children. A piece of her shinbone cracked so badly it had to be removed, which made her left leg shorter than her right. Her parents shipped her far away for help, where she stayed with Aunt Eileen (now dead of breast cancer just like her sister, Callie's mother) and her husband, a university professor, also childless at this point, in their upper-middle class home in Boston. The best doctors in the area worked with reconstruction and rehabilitation, a lucky service to have decades ago. Maggie once told her she regretted not having a sister around to talk to. Callie couldn't reply. Maggie wanted to drag her into another argument about why they weren't any closer as siblings—a discussion neither of them could ever win.

Every Christmas Callie tries to send Maggie something from her past, or her mother's past, something to remind them that they're family, related and bonded by blood. Callie fondles the red and green threads of the quilt's pattern and wonders when she'll send it away to her sister.

* * *

In the afternoon, when her steps have been cleared of ice, and salt sprinkled to stop slips and falls, Callie, booted up, walks down 9th Street and cuts over to Commercial Ave and through the town's main historic block, past the Cap Sante Inn and the closed bakery, wheat and flour growing too expensive for the bakery to remain open, all the way to the bright and rigid Safeway (with her limp, her uneven legs, Callie tries to walk each day—John was a walker too, loved the journeys they took)—the changing storefronts in the historic part of Anacortes keeps her mindset in the past and fogs her thoughts; there used to be a family grocery nestled between the old theater building and a long absent video store. She wonders about other people she doesn't see anymore, the store owners, clerks, the openings and closings, shakes the melancholy fragments in her head away as Safeway's automatic doors open at her approach. She clutches her shopping basket and steps among the mounds of hothouse tomatoes, leaf lettuce, and avocados with a sense of impending doom. A flittering worry takes hold and makes her pick two cans of lentil soup off the shelf without thinking. Terry, the bag boy, gives Callie a cheerful smile when she declines help to her nonexistent car, and says, "You be careful on your walk home."

Callie decides to buy another novel at Watermark Book Co. on the return trip, another mystery by Tana French, someone else whose books she devours, and then decides to buy three more gift copies for Carmel, Harriet, and Mary Lou—she loves giving books at Christmas. It was about time they formed their own book club, and maybe this would be the jumpstart moment. She thinks about the bracelet while the bookstore clerk giftwraps the books. Callie's usually so good at solving the crimes, and this thought pulls her mind in confused directions as she plots the methodical course she took with the bracelet. The snow picks up and she nearly slips crossing M Avenue, where she cuts to the right towards her house. Once home, she places the books and groceries on the counter and puts them away while the images fly, unrevealing the location.

It's her sister she's worrying over. And the present. Then more images come to mind. And somehow she remembers spring days, strolling arm in arm with John, talking to him as he held her hand on their way down the shoreline to take the Guemes Ferry just to get out of the house, the five-minute ferry leading to nearby Guemes Island's only restaurant for their famous fish special and a bowl of clam chowder.

"Look at the swans, Callie. They're making a nest in the reeds. I've never seen them here before. They usually congregate in the fields closer to La Conner," John said to her, pointing out the large white birds at the entrance to a preserved shoreline area. "They mate for life," and John winked as if telling her a joke, and Callie hit his arm telling him she was in on the joke. The distant memory sneaks across her mind and somehow tightens Callie up, makes her jaw ache, and her eyes scan every inch in front of her feet and her cane.

The gold ring she sent to Maggie years ago—she concentrates on that, gets back to the matter at hand, whisks John away. Set with diamonds. The ring used to be her mother's. The bracelet she found in a store in Fairhaven. She's pretty sure the store's called Rooster's Antiques, or something about a farm, the place just south of Bellingham's main city district. The bracelet went with the ring. A perfect match.

Callie climbs the stairs to her room, opens her jewelry box and takes out a small tin filled with tissue. There the ring sat idle for years, and when she brought it to the light the stones glimmered. Now the ring box of her mother's is empty, and Callie can't remember why she kept the tin, why she didn't send it to her sister with the ring. It doesn't make any sense to her, but she must've wanted the tin case as a reminder—her mother's image appears and disappears so quickly that Callie lets out a breath as if just spooked. Callie remains in her room the rest of the day sleeping and reading; the jewelry box stays against her chest until she wakes to start water boiling for tea.

She tells herself the bracelet is only misplaced; hiding the way small children do while playing in a deep wood. Christmas is less than a week away, and Callie wants to mail the package to Maggie tomorrow so it arrives on the eve.

After heating a bowl of soup and corn from the freezer—always corn—she again concentrates on the near and distant past. The family farm now lost to wealthy cattle barons from Denver who bought it for fifty cents on the dollar, still enough to make her father happy. Her father remains proud. She viewed the family farm as if it always had a shroud of darkness overhead—never remembered how she landed in front of the tractor one fateful day—the specific memories of the accident a blackness she can never pierce. Her father drove the tractor and didn't see her. How could that be? Could she have tripped? She wasn't lame then. She never brought up the family farm, always kept her conversations light when calling her dad in Arizona—"You're learning how to play bridge? That's so great, Dad. Who yelled at you for sitting in the wrong seat at the cafeteria? You tell those ladies to mind their own business and keep their hands to themselves." Retirement-home bingo days. Her father didn't want to come to Anacortes, to live in one of the assisted living centers on the island even though they are some of the best in the country, or so the literature says. Callie slips the image of her family's losses into a dark recess in her mind and begins to make a checklist:

1. Her coat pockets are empty. She searches them. Even in places she knows there's no reason for her to have put the bracelet, she scans these places again and again, sometimes two and three times.

2. She scours the old green Ford Mustang with the white convertible top in case the bracelet dropped, even though Callie knows she would've found it by now if it'd been in the car. She washes and vacuums it once a week, inside and out, just like John used to do.

3. The living room: under couches, easy chairs and in the end table drawers, nothing in the canisters on the mantle except matches and a deck of cards.

4. Her hall closet light blinks on when Callie opens it. She sees the shoes first, and most of them are John's. She picks up one of his church shoes; they used to go twice a year, Christmas and Easter, and that was enough for John, a habit from his own upbringing, and Callie looks at the clean black sole and remembers when she bought them for his birthday, and how he never had the stamina to wear them

for more than an hour. Her fingers slide across the leather. She remembers her husband's feet and all the times she washed them and cleaned him when he couldn't move—all the miles they walked together, a winnowing thought shaking a bit of her gloom away. Before he died, Callie hovered an inch from his face and said, "I love you." He touched her hand, moving with the pain and repeated her words back. And the clothes are a reminder. She can't give them away. Five years passed and the clothes always help her remember John in happier moments. Of course Callie's life moves forward. She discovered her solitary existence without John is a burden, and she wants to believe in a higher power the way she was raised, and thinks about going to the upcoming Christmas service and then continuing on with weekly visits, but doubts creep into her mind, a scar weeping, and she can't remove the clothing, the western books; even John's shaving kit remains in the third drawer of the vanity. So many friends of hers cautioned her to give John's belongings away, told her this is better for her mental fortitude, and Callie would then change the subject of their conversation after saying, "Please don't worry so much about me."

Callie places her husband's shoe next to its mate and then rummages through the front hanging coats, jackets, and dress shirts John stored there. She pulls out her light-weather coat for the fourth time and turns it inside out. A receipt from Watermark bookstore—more mystery books read and then boxed and sent to Maggie—falls from an inside pocket and twirls to the ground. Callie picks it up and throws it away.

Her list continues:

5. Her bedroom's the last place to check: the dresser, where John's office socks sprinkle in with her patterned socks and hose. She tries to think about the bracelet, retrace her steps from Rooster's Antiques, the return drive to her

house, where she put the small brown paper bag for safe keeping, but can't come up with anything in the convertible. It was a nice day, full spring sunshine, the top down as she drove home on the scenic Chuckanut Drive, and stopped at The Farmhouse for an early supper—could the wind have taken the bag and blown it into Puget Sound, right over the cliff? Preposterous, but there was nothing under her mattress; she looked just for the sake of looking there. Nothing in her closet except more dresses, which she goes through another time, checking pockets and the floor beneath in case, just in case.

Callie feels her pulse rise when she stops searching, and puts a finger to her throat. She makes her way out of the closet, into her adjacent bathroom and stares at her weary face in the mirror as if to conjure answers from a crystal globe. She moves her fingers to the lines surrounding her eyes and traces them slowly to her mouth. John always rubbed her cheeks and found pressure points beneath her eyes and above her curving lips where he massaged to relieve tension. In the mirror she thinks she sees John's hands over her own, skeletal, spotted, ripe with wrinkles, and she starts to cry into them.

* * *

After a warm bath, Callie pulls a flannel nightgown on and climbs into bed. She'll return to her search in the morning. When the telephone rings, it snaps her out of her list-making and she picks up the receiver and says, "Hello?"

It's Maggie calling to ask Callie how she's getting along this Christmas. Callie updates Maggie about her teaching job and the levy that didn't pass on the first vote. "Things are going to be pretty tight in this town, Maggie," Callie says, "until I know I still have my classroom." Her voice comes across scratchy and almost feverish.

"The kids are fine and wonder when they'll see their aunt again," Maggie says. "I'm very sorry about your school's position. I wish I could do something."

It's the way Maggie always talks to Callie. Never listening to Callie or responding to her daily worries until she talks about her children or her family or what's happening in Colorado. This is Christmas. This is her job. This is why Maggie votes like their dad, and they never talk politics anymore; the family knows better. Callie doesn't want to get into another senseless argument. Many of her friends follow different politicians across the abyss, and they think her own opinions don't amount to much either. With more time spent in their mother's presence, Maggie kept topics of conversation to small stuff, seldom ever wanted to dig below the surface, learned from her mother: just be polite, which makes Callie's own facile mental questioning and creative drive, paired with her physical rigidity, all the more oppositional, and, how they dance around serious subjects, laughable. Callie wants to say she's sorry, to spout her real concerns and tell Maggie about the bracelet, but her throat closes and she coughs, holding the receiver away — she wishes she could scream.

Maggie keeps talking about her plans and the children being accomplished boarders, amazing computer and gaming experts (wanting new snowboarding equipment, clothing, computer games), gift suggestions without really being gift suggestions, and how smart all of them really are, how their eldest, George, may receive an athletic scholarship in soccer, how much it costs to keep him in the elite field each year. She doesn't mention academic pursuits, but her two nephews and one niece, Sheila, described by their mother as budding geniuses, often make Callie smile. Callie loves them. It's her sister who irritates with her bubbling-over cheer. Callie clears her throat, listens, and thinks about all the kids she's taught, and how most of them would run from the school, turn their backs, if it wasn't mandatory, and how little they're learning now.

"That's nice, Maggie," Callie says. "I hope they love what I sent them." The week before, Callie wrapped, boxed up, and shipped books, the hottest titles of the moment, and included a couple t-shirts for each child with orcas (whale-watching tours being a must-do tourist activity in the area), otters, in playful, gamboling native designs. She didn't want to wait in case the bracelet never materialized — deprive her nephews and niece of a gift from her come Christmas morning.

"I'm sure they will, but they've been so hyperactive I wish I could put them on work detail up in the North Pole...I want you to know that we're planning a trip out your way to see you this summer. If it's in the budget and all. It's been two years, right?"

Callie says, "I haven't sent your present yet. It's almost too late now and I feel awful." She hears one of her nephews shouting in the background. A couple seconds pass.

"What's that? I'm sorry I missed what you just said. Sheila hit Mark and, honest to God, the little weasel bit her arm. I had to tear them apart. You know how kids can be." Mark had always been Callie's favorite, and this thought made her sad—kids changing before their parents' very eyes, an aunt calculating how much they've changed physically and emotionally since the last visit.

"I said I hope you have a merry Christmas and I'll be thinking of you. Getting together this summer would be wonderful."

"Don't worry about your job. It'll turn out all right. You'll see. I love you."

"I love you too, Maggie. Merry Christmas."

They hang up at the same time. After she extinguishes the light, Callie snuggles into her blankets. She and her sister didn't bring up the fact that neither of them planned

to go down to Arizona to spend Christmas with their
father. He didn't want them there. ("I'm fine right where
I am. Callie, I don't need you fussing about with nothing
to do and spending all your money on me. Maggie, you
come see me when the kids have spring break…they can
swim in the pool.") His two daughters never went against
his wishes—and there's guilt in Callie's worrying. Stuck
in the same room with each other, Callie always faces the
etched-in guilt in her dad's eyes; he still blames himself
for her scars, her shortened leg, and will not let the wound
close. Callie sent him a new pair of slippers, easy to just
step into, and the Booker Prize-winning novel, *The Narrow
Road to the Deep North*, about the construction of the
Thailand-Burma Death Railway in World War II, that and
more, something her father would get lost in—these gifts
shuttling on their way only a couple days past—Merry
Christmas, Dad. Love, Callie.

*   *   *

Her sleep breaks in the early morning, and Callie continues
to picture John from her dream. The coldness of the air in
the room slaps the vision to pieces, and she can only recol-
lect bits: John sitting on his riding lawn mower wearing his
red jacket, waving to Callie. Long ago, the day she first saw
him in line at the Puget Sound Bank, before she'd completed
the coursework for her teaching certificate up at Western
University, when she was working as a teller, hoping he'd
end up in front of her. The expression on his face passing in
her sleep—film under water.

Callie's vision blurs until she shakes her head. She takes
her cane and goes downstairs. The *Anacortes American* is on
her doorstep, shiny with ice particles. Weekly news of job-
less people, farmers out of luck and still earning the same
prices for grain and corn they did in the thirties and how

sustainable farming is making inroads, letters to the editor rallying a plea to the town stating what dire circumstances everyone is in for: "Do you want your children's education to languish because the school can't sustain a sports program, foreign languages, physical education classes, clubs, art, and high school bus transportation? Please vote yes next February, and until then think of your children."

It'll pass this time, Callie hopes. How could it not? After Christmas, people will tighten their purse strings, but they won't want their kids to suffer. So many people are out of work as it is.

Her skin raises gooseflesh and she walks to the hall closet to cover herself in a warm coat, one of John's wool Pendleton coats, and the answer reveals itself, robbed from her memory for so long that she's not sure if her mind's playing tricks on her.

Callie remembers the April day she drove along Chuckanut Drive, the most scenic road in Washington State, right along the coastline, curvy thrills, to visit another teacher and to see the current wows in her favorite art galleries. She made sure there was enough time to drop in for an hour's browsing at Village Books (one of her favorite bookstores off-island), and to search through antique stores in Fairhaven. It was sunny, she remembers the warmth that day, the wind blowing through her hair on the drive home, but she awoke to a chill that morning. Long forgotten, a mundane detail, as her coat stayed put because of the frost on the ground. She decided to wear one of John's jackets in case she could put the 1972 Mustang's convertible top down (John treated his green car with the white top like a favored child and so did Callie now) on the drive home and grabbed one from the closet.

Her fingers push through the clothing until a second layer reveals itself. She wore John's large red jacket; the one with the big pockets; the one the wind couldn't cut through and the rain couldn't puncture; the one he wore in her dream, where John smiled at her, saying he was in on the joke, and Callie lets out a braying laugh. Callie rifles the pockets and turns them out. The small brown paper package falls into her hand and Callie takes the bracelet from within. She makes a nest on the closet floor with John's clothing. She sinks down and rests, comfortable, on her husband's shirts, hunting jackets and shoes. She smells the oldness. Callie puts the bracelet around her wrist—a gift that fits, calms her anxious mind. Callie knows John's beside her, all around her, and the bracelet is his present to her, a comfort as she touches the gold and runs her fingertips across the intricate array of diamonds. Callie says thank you, out loud, and then tells John she'll never take it off.

When the post office opens, Callie is first in line. She walks right up to the postal clerk's desk, her limp obvious to everyone behind her, places the large box on the counter, and smiles.

"Merry Christmas, Callie. Are the contents breakable? Would you like to insure this today?" She loves living in a town where everyone knows her.

"No, thank you," Callie says as she pays the bill, "happy holidays to you." Callie turns and walks out the building. She's happy as a hopeful relief eases her mind. She thinks about how much her sister will cherish their mother's Christmas quilt as much as she did.

The End

EVERYONE WANTS ME TO

Arlene

AT SEVEN A.M. ON A DRIZZLING, icy day in early March, the North Central airliner approached Willow Run at a speed that rattled its occupants. Arlene kept her fear and possible yipping screams bottled up inside. This flight was supposed to be for her, to bring her family back together again. If her mother asked her why she fidgeted so much, Arlene would tell her the plane's altitude drops and subtle lifts made her feel loopy.

"It's the same as a roller coaster. You love seeing those, remember? The wooden one we saw when we visited the ocean park, up and down, baby. Nothing to be 'fraid of." Her mother asked the flight attendant for a comfort bag early on, and this remained close at hand on their tray table. Arlene didn't like staring at it and imagining herself stricken uncontrollably, reaching for the bag too late. Shrieking.

Air travel remained a new and impossible-to-reach shiny fantasy for most of these passengers, a startling convenience in 1953 for the masses, but built for the well-mannered gentry.

The class system in changeable flux, most passengers felt lucky; few felt afraid, the phobia of flying, the clinical diagnosis name at that moment a seed buried under cold dark earth.

Wind swept freezing rain against the portholes, and made them near impossible to see out of. Except for the gloom. That was ever-present. With the runways slicked up, icicles hung from the control tower. Several of the passengers had made connections in Tucson from L.A. These were the red-eyed precursor to today's businessmen in loosened ties and wrinkled blue suits. Another stop in Chicago crowded the compartments with people of middle-class upbringing who lived in places closer to Detroit: Chelsea, Flint, Bay City, and Saginaw. All of the people felt a bit grumpy and puffy-eyed after the night's passage, their faces slack like the ice pools on the runway.

In the second row of the first-class section a thin-boned woman with too much makeup, reapplied before touchdown, patted the knee of Arlene next to her.

"All over, Arlene. You've got to be strong, for me. Be a big girl."

Arlene lowered her head and kept silent. The airplane rocked and skidded, moved across the tarmac on its way to the terminal. The sky pressed down on them, a brick to mortar.

"Isn't it wonderful? It sure is great to be back. You'll love the house. It's so huge, you can get lost in it. I'll come find you." Arlene's mother said, even though she realized Arlene hadn't stepped foot in Michigan in years. She was a teenager now, and the distance between them had twisted over time and separation. "What do you say we stop for ice cream or a soda on the way home? I'm sure Daddy won't mind."

Arlene remained silent as the airplane lights came on and people jumped up, jostling one another trying to procure their hand luggage from in front of their seats. It's too cold for ice cream, Arlene thought. After bending down so that she faced the teenager, a stewardess asked if Arlene had enjoyed the flight, and wasn't it an exciting first-time flying experience?

She shook her head no because she knew that the desert landscape's sunshine would always beckon to her.

"Oh. She's not feeling well. I've got to get her home."

"Well I hope you're better soon and fly with North Central again," the stewardess said, and then glanced at a passenger skirting past her. "Sir? Sir? You forgot your gloves."

Arlene unbuckled her seat belt, stood up and stretched her arms above her head. Her legs had sleep pins pricking her skin, and she twitched with discomfort. Her mother was trying to decide what to do with her. They were meeting Barry, Arlene's father, at the gate; he was probably waiting for them now.

* * *

That was when it all started. I think. Back then I didn't want to return to Michigan. I suppose I could've cried and screamed harder in Tucson, made my grandmother's guilt rack her into bitter grief, but who really knows if my life would've turned out any different, taken some other turn for the better, worse, or remained the same.

Getting off the airplane and descending into the grizzly cold Michigan day made me miss my grandparents' house even more. Their one-story wood ranch house was painted a dark green, and boulders and large cacti sprouted and stayed silent around the front yard. In the back of the house was an orange tree orchard, and I'd help pick the oranges and place them in boxes to take to the buyer. Everyone had water systems and oranges growing in their yards. Not many people know that oranges can grow in the middle of the desert. I learned to protect your water, that it was the most important substance on the planet beyond blood. Water formed tears.

I wanted to stay there with the parched wind and wrinkled neighbors who took me swimming in the park. I even missed the scorpions, how intelligently clever their evolution, getting into everything. I slept in a bed with kerosene cans placed all around and under the legs so the scorpions would fall to their deaths. I'd watch them and nine times out of ten want to help them.

You see, I had no say in the matter, no one really wanted me, and I think this is fine, really, I think this is okay. My mother had me when she wasn't prepared for the responsibility. The person I'm supposed to call my father is, was, a prick, a prickly cactus, one of the tall belligerent ones who lorded their girth over every other denizen in front of him to the horizon and beyond.

And that is fine also. He wanted to send me to camp the first year I was born. My mother told me this when I started going to the Bloomfield Hills Summer Camp for Girls at age five, before the Arizona departure. She laughed lightly and said he was teasing, but I knew she was faking, because I *knew* my father would've sent me to a Suckling Babes of Bloomfield Hills Long Term Camp if he could've.

After my mother's parents arrived by car the fall of my eighth year, for two week's vacation, when Tucson temperatures still hit the upper nineties, they wanted to take me back to Arizona with them. I heard them tell my mother I wasn't happy and didn't have much to do here in Michigan; they meant I was neglected. My father was gung-ho for the idea and actually pretended to be nice to me, bought me a small pink suitcase. Each Christmas, loads of wrapped gifts arrived on my grandparents' doorstep.

"Your parents are on a cruise to Egypt," my grandmother said, and she didn't have to say she thought my father was the most self-centered jackass she'd ever wished her daughter had never stumbled into, the pretty girl catching the covetous bird's fancy. My mother was a knockout, a doll, and his plaything. She sent photos of the pyramids and hieroglyphics one year, shared weekly postcards from other trips, other Christmases — polka festivals in Munich, the Mona Lisa smile, bangers and mash for Santa's Irish feast. When I first arrived in Arizona, at the time, I thought it was going to be for a week, maybe two at the most, but five years went by like a flash flood. When grandfather died in the sixth year of my sabbatical, my parents decided to put grandmother in a retirement home; she was losing her memory, the past becoming her present once more, scalding at times, and I wondered about her own upbringing, something she'd never revealed, not even once. It sounded like it was also filled with spite, her father dying in some war, her mother desperate to find another husband she could cling to, make dinners for, sew uniforms, mend socks, get knocked up again with. A half sibling sprouted and abandoned the nest to explore Vermont, unknown to me. Owned a maple syrup company, not that she'd ever remember his name or the name of his business. In her forgetful state she told me secrets and I'll take them to my own grave. My mother came out to make arrangements, sell the ranch house and the orange tree orchard, place grandmother into a service-oriented hospital with good nursing care. I told my mother there was nothing wrong with Grandmother, but she looked away and started to cry. She told me later my father made her do it. She'd never forgive herself for locking her mother away in a home in Arizona. I kept asking why we couldn't take her with us to Michigan until my mother, her oval face twisting, screamed at me to be quiet for God's sake, not another word.

*   *   *

He didn't look happy. His dark lips formed a permanent scowl. He thought it was Arlene's fault when the airplane arrived fifty minutes late, that she had somehow caused a disruption in the clouds above Michigan. Walking slowly behind her mother, Arlene kept her head down. Run away, she thought. Just run away.

The tennis shoes Arlene had on were dusty brown. Her fading daisy-print dress came down to her knees. Threads hung limply and poked from the seams. Pulled along by her mother, Arlene glanced up at her father's face. He stared back, brown eyes shifting, and told her to stop holding everybody up.

"There are some new rules in my house. You'll follow them." There wasn't any debate. The *or else* was explicitly clear.

Since his meeting started in an hour, he handed Marion enough money for a taxi ride back to the house in Bloomfield Hills and told them he'd be back late that night and they shouldn't wait up for him. He also told Arlene not to get into trouble.

When Barry entered his office in Birmingham, he went straight to his bottom desk drawer and pulled out his stashed bottle of cheap scotch and drank and drank until his secretary knocked, asked him if he wanted her to stay, to help ease the pain in his shoulders, and told him to have a good night after he said, "Not tonight, Rachel. Maybe tomorrow."

*   *   *

Everyone expected so much for me, said I had it so easy living the high life in the big brick mansion. I was supposed to keep myself busy, learn to love solitude. All the time. I felt like I was on stage from when I woke up in the morning to when I went to sleep at night. Even when I went to sleep, though, I knew, I was sure I was being judged in some unknown way. He woke me most mornings with incoherent yelling. Mother kept me out of his way until he left for work, but she wouldn't do anything else for me. I was now more of a chore for her. A thirteen-year-old girl no one wanted around. In Tucson I felt needed. When grandfather died of a heart attack, I felt betrayed. My father, the one who never calls me Arlene, always you or girl or trouble, put my grandmother in a hospital. Marion, my marionette mother, came to set it up in person and take me back. But it was really my father, The Puppeteer, who pulled the puppet strings; set it up from a distance and made Mother come fetch me like a wayward pet dog. The next year they told me grandmother died in her sleep. I could picture her withering away in a strange room, a fan crackling in one corner shifting the heat. Even distorted by dementia, I want to believe my grandmother understood what she'd lost, that she simply gave up, ready to cross a distant horizon line—join her lost love. It's not right. They were too young.

There was too much of that feeling in the house, but I can't say I didn't enjoy anything. I was young and learned where to be at the right time. More importantly, I learned where not to be—I could get lost in that house and no one would ever find me. I couldn't mention my grandparents in their presence anymore. That was a new rule.

On a day I'll always remember after trying so hard to black it out, one moment from the past hit my dreams like a shot, and upon waking I pieced things together. When I was seven, almost a whole year before my grandparents decided to take me away and show me a never-changing desert landscape, I snuck out of the house before my parents woke up and wandered into the back woods. It was warm, but a cool wind passed through new poplars and oaks that stood in the shadows of the older trees. My father forbade me to go into the woods behind the house. He said a girl shouldn't play where strangers could hurt her. I never saw anyone but Philby in the woods, and he wasn't a stranger. I'd go anyway, almost every day. Sometimes Philby, the tight-faced slow boy who lived down my street, would meet me there and we'd play war games, cowboys and prairie wives, and Lassie down the well, and Penelope Pitstop tied to train tracks.

Philby was a lonely boy. He wasn't weak or anything; he mostly entertained himself. I asked him about his parents from time to time. He would shrug his shoulders and change the subject. I thought we were soul mates, and sometimes I'd pretend we were Dickensian orphans sold at birth to unforgiving grifters or Bolsheviks in search of a new Communist Party. The object of the game was to make Philby conform. The red scare blared out at us every morning on the news, pressed into us by our parents. During these imaginary plays, passing the time away, Philby would also pretend, join me when I told him why I was building a fort down near the creek.

It was our secret place. I named it Orphan Sanctuary, and Philby scrawled this on a piece of wood and nailed it to a tree outside the blanket-covered entrance. I stole them out of a storage closet. They were on the bottom of a pile of worn wool blankets. No one noticed. I'd always been a scrounger.

My mother knew I went into the woods but she didn't tell my father. She pulled me aside, though, and told me to be careful and only go out there when he was working.

That morning, I wanted to try something new. This is just one instance of my disobedience. No excuses. I took the pain and suffered with it for years; even today the memories curdle inside and twist my feelings into a bitterness I take out on anyone I meet on the street. Maybe the crack in my head widened at this moment, shattered my thoughts to icy bracing bits of insanity. I blacked this part out for so long.

Philby was away with his parents on a trip to Florida. Whisk — and he was away for weeks. I carried on alone. If you walked along the creek past Orphan Sanctuary and turned left where the creek divided, one side becoming a small waterfall, you'd come to the start of a tree farm, waist-high Christmas trees lined up in rows all the way to the distant hill, beyond to the highway, and ending at a deep gorge—my favorite place in the world to walk through, for the scent, the holiday Douglas fir soldiers preparing for seasonal battle. I had Christmas dreams in summertime. The gorge fascinated me too. At the bottom of the pit, earth-movers and trucks pried and pulled out huge boulders and roots. The walls of the ravine slanted on three sides. The developers left one side gentler so trucks could drive down. It wasn't a straight drop of thirty feet. There was a slight roll to it.

There was no one around because it was Sunday. Philby and I had always wanted to go down and explore the machines, crawl on the large piles of earth, find out what was hidden in all the long piping stacked like toothpicks, play king of the mountain, but we didn't have the nerve to try and slide down the side of the chasm. Neither of us admitted it would be a lot easier to walk around to the far side of the pit and walk down the gently sloping side. It was a dare no one wanted to try when someone else was watching. Being alone, I dared myself, and accepted the challenge.

I stood at the edge listening to the birds, yellow finches and loons, flying in the trees building nests and glanced all around me to make sure I was really alone. Putting my right foot forward was a mistake; my upper body crouched for balance, I made the first step. With a jerk, my knees buckled out from under me immediately, the ground shifting, I swore, rolling soil like flour through a sieve. I fell sideways, hitting my left shoulder hard. I rolled, bounced out, but I felt weightless because of how steep it was. My head struck a piece of driftwood halfway down the slope, and then I hit something else harder and blacked out. A few seconds, minutes ticking by, maybe even more than a few. Time passed on and I wasn't sure how long I spent unconscious

at the bottom of the pit among the earthmovers. The sun
shone high to the left. When I awoke, my ears ringing, I felt
two great pains. The back of my head bled and eventually
dried in a matte-like mess, the blood trickling slowed, and
tickling pressure squeezed my eyes shut and I couldn't
catch my breath. I tried to stand and couldn't bring my
left arm around for support without nausea, seeing purple
spots verging on turning to black void, shunting dull aches
blooming into splinters of sharpness. My arm throbbed
under me with bleak knots of pain, pulled back in awkward,
unnatural alignment, tight on the ground like some numb
pillow. I knew I was crying, but no one was around to hear.
I must've sat there for another half hour, futile tears mess-
ing with the dust and dirt across my skin.

Stumbling up on my feet caused ripples, crashing waves
of pain to sliver deeper. I tilted my head to look at the top
of the gorge. Too far away now. Climbing back the same
way I came down was futile. I stepped my way carefully
around the machines and made it up the easier gradient.
On my way home, crossing the creek, I thought of what
would happen to me when I returned. My left arm hung
limply, useless, at my side and the shoulder swelled into a
mass tender to my exploring touch. Inch by sensitive inch,
the fingers of my left hand turned a dark ripe plum. All
feeling deserted me, and I welcomed this new numbness.

*　*　*

Barry and Marion Galena studied each other in the kitchen
while they drank coffee. He watched her as she went for the
cream and sugar, frozen smile and wispy hair still trying
to tell him something. The current maid was off doing God
knew what, and this irked both of them to no end. When
they were mad at each other, circling each other like nasty
cats in a ring, they tended to take their frustrations out on

the maids—they didn't last long in their employ. Marion thought about all the mornings during the week when she had the kitchen to herself, when he was off to work, drinking already, something without scent, covert showers attempting to cover up something else (not always succeeding), a different perfume, animalistic rutting, the smell of another woman. She'd known about it for three months now and refused to bring it up. She thought about her future, growing colder, a frozen rabbit in its hutch, forgotten, until the images of Barry with someone else remained buried behind opaque glass. He watched her, deep in his own thoughts about being tied down, festering in a relationship he'd never wanted in the first place, forced by another hand.

Arlene opened the back door and leaned against the frame. Tears welled and smeared dirt down her cheeks. Marion's first thought: my child's a mud-ball. Arlene didn't want to tell them the truth. She could practice telling little white lies, fail until she got it right. Anything she could think up would be better than the truth. She could say she didn't remember what happened, that the knock to her head caused her to lose her memory, that the stranger her father warned her about had finally made an appearance, grabbed her and pushed her down and she couldn't get up, that he was still on top of her. Barry stared at Arlene and his face became a red fire. She would ruin his day as the fire of rage sparked by her obvious disobedience burnt into his skin and exploded the image he was trying to build of safe seductive secrets, and longing, a powerful lust for a woman he met in a bar on Livernois Avenue. Getting out of this mistake, how to reverse his errors, made his bitterness bloom into hatred towards both his wife and daughter. Marion pushed her chair back, spilled drops of coffee when she put her cup on the counter, and came quickly over to her daughter. She put her hand on Arlene's bad shoulder and Arlene almost passed out again.

Her mother asked her how this happened. Her tone masked a wave of wary believability. He did this somehow, and she turned to look at Barry. She guided Arlene onto a kitchen chair, and Arlene wondered why her father was calling her by her name for the first time in memory.

Arlene stuttered, pierced the morning air as she said she couldn't feel her hand. It was an illusion in front of her, dead weight.

"I'll tell you what happened. She disobeyed me again. I told you she never listens." And there was more; Barry believed she wanted to make his life miserable, a purposeful, disrespecting thrill. "Stop your crying. I won't have liars in my house."

"Barry. Barry. She's really hurt."

"I don't care. It's what she deserves for lying to me. You've been faking everything too, Mary, for that Goddamned matter, so I don't want to hear it."

Arlene's eyes rolled white in the sockets, and she started to slide off the wooden chair. Marion screamed, "Help me with her. Help me put her in the car." Barry sneered at his wife and threw his coffee cup onto the floor. Ceramic shards flew against the speckled tile. This was the break, the new beginning, and Marion knew it was over for her and Arlene; she wouldn't take anymore, she'd make her plans and move out like a shadow.

"Don't ever tell me what to do. She's your child. Not mine. You used her to trap me. I never wanted her. Get that through your head, Mary, or…"

"Or what?" That vituperative brio, the tone, was enough. She stared at him, and, for once, she made him back down.

His silence made Marion wish she hadn't fought back. She started to cry, joining into the wet, heavy, invisible atmosphere. Not because of how awful he was, but because she was powerless to stop it. She'd always been the weak one, always needed someone to intervene on her behalf. He knew that when he married her. Knew she'd fall before him.

He gripped Arlene's right arm and pulled her to her feet. She moaned and let her weight fall against his chest. As he carried her out to the car, he said, "I don't want to hear a peep out of you." Marion understood he was speaking to her as well as Arlene. They were locked in with a monster, Marion thought. A monster she helped play a part in creating.

*   *   *

I can remember the nurse strapping a black scratchy cuff around my right arm, pumping a small black balloon and watching her take a reading, marking a check on a form, numbers on a chart. My left hand now had a blackish tint to it, and the dark plum color was creeping up my wrist. A doctor came in right away and prodded my shoulder with his finger. He didn't have to ask me if it hurt. My father told him to get on with it. The doctor asked the nurse if she would show my father out to the waiting room where my mother stayed, pushed in a chair against a wall. I think he wanted to feel my pain so he could use it later, store it up inside of him to remind me of what I did. Words were passed; they were angry words. The mention of security and professionalism circled back and forth. Then the doctor leaned down to where my bloody hair matted against my head, close to my ear, and asked me if I wanted my father there for support. The words came out fast before I could take them back: He isn't my father. He said I wasn't his. I don't want him.

My mother told me later that he left the hospital without telling her where he was going. She'd tried calling home and his office too many times as hours passed. No reply. She told me all this hours later. After my arm, shoulder, and hand received x-rays along with my skull to check for fractures and dislocation—a mild concussion, more than mild, dizzy,

head-injury protocols. A break in my left shoulder had
stopped the flow of blood to my arm. The doctor manipulated
the collarbone to bring my arm forward. Screaming at anyone
and everyone in my little curtain-drawn cubicle was all I
could do. A nurse put a shoulder halter and a sling under my
arm and told me to lie back; rest a little bit. We have to keep
an eye on you for a couple hours to make sure that bump to
the head the doctor sewed up is really a bump and not too
serious of a concussion or a closed head injury of any kind.

I shut my eyes and thought about what was going to
happen to me. The air filled with dusty spirals and the future
beckoned and this image became important to me, how I'd
live once I got back home, keeping the stalking tiger in its cage.

It was an easy thing to see. After the fall, my life would
change; I could be the same and yet different. Inside I
felt betrayed by everything: life fate luck father mother
being born birthdays gifts years passing Christmas trees
unadorned soldiers wondering if I had anyone else Philby
the perpetual neighbor boy for being gone and not telling
me about how good his parents really were to him because
he knew mine were lousy the doctor the nurse who held me
down while I struggled when I saw the needle come closer
to numb my head so that the stitches could be sewn anyone
who helped everyone else get better before me taking care
of business and not worrying the man who owned the
land with the earth-movers who came and questioned me
because I wasn't supposed to be where I was and didn't
anyone ever tell me to stay off private property and his false
sympathy in light of a possible law suit action to secure
justice in a county court of law my father was interested
in pressing because of the money and not make a fool of
myself you're old enough to face some responsibility are
you happy at home do you feel depressed and do you really
think your parents are happy every time you disobey them
the school the man who walks me across the street stopping

traffic with his bright red sign the same man who once lifted up my skirt to see my underwear when there were no cars and no one else around to stop him while he was supposed to stop traffic and himself and it was weird and I cried because I felt it was wrong like everyone is saying I'm wrong to want privacy and be able to go where I want to when I want to and them saying how can we trust you when you deliberately go against our wishes trespassing and hurting yourself you're lucky you didn't break your leg who would find you or help you then Arlene and the bills this is going to cost us will be taken out of your allowance until you are old enough to fly on your own out of the nest once and forever all alone is where they want me with no friends to influence me or my decision to stay away from my father as much as possible which I try to do but sometimes it's so hard and I feel like I'm suffocated being swallowed up by him and all his rules and regulations that are only meant to keep me in line a prisoner in my own house which really isn't my house or my place of birth or anywhere on the face of the earth for that matter letting everyone see me for what I am a runaway but not a victim because I will run my life the way I want to and not the way anyone or my father or my mother or everyone wants me to.

Marion

Marion could only believe in one idea at a time or a debilitating anxiety threatened to overwhelm her, shake her inner harmony—a state of bliss was often unknown to her. She strove to finish one chore completely before marking this off a never-ending list. She believed tasks became easier to accomplish, even those of the imaginary kind, the wishes to change someone beyond herself, ease tantrums, rages, and, later on in her married years, the need to leave her bed. When she was shopping for new shoes nothing else could stop her progress. So the education she received from the University of Michigan was second in line to her main goal, her main idea: finding a husband, the word *good* was implied, but not well thought out. There were a lot of other women like her at school, and they'd eye each other at the library or in class when caught looking at the same man across the room instead of concentrating on the professor's lecture, even though some of the professors looked just as intently at some of the women. She couldn't become brazen, that would be too much, and lowering the top of her blouse like Samantha, Regina, or the head of one of the preppy sororities, Layla, wasn't in her playbook.

She counted on everyone else to make her life wonderful, and friends would always include Marion in their lives. She had a charm, a glowing and burgeoning self confidence that up to this point had never blossomed, even going steady in high school with one of the star jocks—looking back, Marion felt her high school years didn't help her at all. She was simply likable, not very likable, in a plain way, one of the girls, part of a happy group of collegiate women laughing and giggling across campus, making young gentlemen turn and catcall in ways that was laughed off, the menacing flattery to be mocked while part of a group. Alone, menace came to the front with ease. Her dorm monitor insisted no one walk alone across campus, and Marion followed orders well.

Given the fact that Marion was only a sophomore when she met Barry Galena, there was a lot of time, on her part, to get to know him better, to make certain decisions about her future, her goal in life.

They met in Angel Hall where Marion and her best friend at the time, Molly Green, were studying for a broadcasting midterm. The people studying in Angel Hall, the building the football players were forced to study in from seven p.m. until ten o'clock, four nights a week, bumped into each other often, around corners, at the drinking fountain, opening exit doors. At the University of Michigan, even back then, the coach was forced to put some emphasis on the academic schedule. Each player had his own tutor depending on what room in Angel Hall he went into that night: one room for calculus, one room for chemistry, English, physiology, economics, or health, and so on down the third and fourth floors of the building.

Marion always studied in Angel because she knew the football team would always be there—she loved jocks, felt safe in their company, comforted by their embraces, part of their glib humor. She took many long study breaks to the drinking fountain, and she would have her mind set on meeting someone on the team and something light and nice to say to that someone, not on how to integrate new communication strategies into the radio business. She was singular in her efforts. Whenever Marion wandered back to her classroom where Molly was busy memorizing theories, she would tease Molly about not being so studious all the time, how she'd never catch a man. They'd collect their notebooks and rush to their dorm before the ten o'clock curfew.

"Don't you want to meet a football player, Molly? You'll pass tomorrow's test easily."

But Molly would laugh and tease Marion about her Mrs. degree.

* * *

I wanted someone to take care of me. It didn't really matter if I fell in love or not. It's what I was taught. The radio shows, the ads, brayed out how to please my man, wear something chic, or act sophisticated. Everyone in my high school, the women who were teachers anyway, tried to act like Marlene Dietrich or Judy Garland (not my contemporaries—we adored Elizabeth Taylor and followed her every

move), with Judy's innocent sweet look, to learn from them
and find out what we've been missing all our lives. When I
first spoke to Barry near the drinking fountain on the third
floor, I knew he was the one for me. I can say that now and
wish to God it wasn't true, but, at the time, I thought writing papers was the most boring thing ever invented, who'd
care in thirty years anyway what I wrote about Emerson.

Of course I knew he was kind of rough: very loud and out-
spoken, a regular Honeymooner. He could be quiet at times,
contemplative even, and moody. I'd say hello and he'd say
how are you and he made me feel wonderful. I can remember
those good times and think about when the cracks appeared.
So many times I tried to glue the chips back in place.

He took me to a bar outside Ann Arbor, closer to Detroit,
the next night. His father had money and gave him a car to
use, which was a big deal back then. I remember drinking
tequila for the first time, shooting down my throat with salt
and bitter lemon, and then a lot of gin. I also remember not
going back to Martha Cook, my dorm, until the next morning. When I opened the door and my roommate, Constance
Disher, pointed to the note on my desk, I knew I was in
trouble. I didn't care if they kicked me out of the all-girl
dorm or not. They didn't. Reprimanded by Mrs. Parkinson,
a sort of "den mother" of the dorm who made sure all the
rules were followed to the letter, I took my licks, apologized,
said it'll never happen again, and raced to the washroom to
clean up before I became messy. No one could be out past
10:00 p.m. except during planned social events like dances
and sorority formals.

Mrs. Parkinson wanted to know where I'd been, and I
told her I got locked out of the dorm and had spent the
night at my friend's dorm and she could call Molly Green
if she didn't believe me. Later, Molly told me she wouldn't
cover for me ever again. We lost contact with each other and
fell in with different crowds. Her crowd made up of book

reports, teachers, and libraries, and mine made up of Barry Galena, football Saturdays, and parties.

After not too much time passed, I found myself losing interest in anything that didn't relate to Barry. I suppose most of my fawning behavior could fall under the term obsession, but I didn't care back then and I don't think I would've even recognized that fact. I could cheat at He-Loves-Me-He-Loves-Me-Not with the best con artists in Michigan, just hand me a daisy. I wasn't mature enough to know how obsequiousness wasn't a desired personality trait, that the other jocks teased Barry about his little shadow, made sucking kissy noises behind our backs, which only made me turn red with fury towards their immaturity; another bad sign since I wasn't turning red with shame.

Today is another story altogether. I agree. I never applied myself back then; always wanted the easy way out, without fighting, but I'm working in a hospital now, helping people, following doctors' orders, talking to people; I'm (really) a good nurse. Arlene is off in school taking after me, having already learned hardness from her father. We, Barry and I, don't see each other at all. He doesn't call me and I don't call him. As soon as I received my nursing degree, I became self-sufficient for the first time in my life. I'll never feel guilty for taking Arlene and walking out.

* * *

Marion set up the entire evening.

Her roommate agreed just this once to cover for her when Mrs. Parkinson called to check the rooms at 11:00. When Barry took her back to his dorm room after the pep rally, she'd give in to his demands.

Barry's strong hand held Marion's wrist and he stared at her tiny fingers. "I want you to stay the night, Mary." He was the only one allowed to call her Mary.

Marion glanced down at the back of his hand, at the veins crisscrossing, and pulled away. She turned her back on him, and said, "Can you help me with my zipper."

It hurt so much (he wasn't gentle even when she told him to be, a first promise broken, a major one, but Marion could overlook most anything), and, later, maybe a minute or two, it all happened so quickly in retrospect, there was no way to stop him once he became rougher. His eyes remained closed. His need grew. He was so much stronger and Marion winced and bit her lip until it bled and she waited, and thought, "let it be over soon." Afterwards, lying side by side, the pressure within her became a numbness and she fell into it, making her plans, knowing that it wasn't entirely her fault, come what may; he and she'd known exactly what they were doing, come what may.

Less than two months later Barry left Ann Arbor and joined the army. School wasn't for him. Mary wasn't for him. She told him about her uncertain fears.

He didn't say goodbye to Marion and she began to plan her future again, possibly with someone new, until she found out for sure she was pregnant. She was back on the third floor of Angel Hall, glancing at the other football players who walked by her open door and talking to the players who knew her as Barry's girl. They felt sorry for her and asked her what she was doing now that Barry was gone. She couldn't tell anyone she was pregnant, and soon she followed Barry's decision and quit school. She went back home to talk to her own doctor. She was still not certain, but a week later she knew for sure and she began to plan all over again.

Barry

When Barry Galena was ten, his father told him the philosophy of life: do whatever you can to stay on top. And that means anything. Never let anyone have the upper hand. Always, always, have the last word. He remained in awe of his father. Barry remained silent in his presence.

As he grew older, Barry learned how right his father was. He entered the University of Michigan on a football scholarship—this was the early 40s and war was there gleaming and coercing young men to fight, beguiling them, scratching every patriotic itch. After every game, no matter if the team had won or lost, Barry would have a couple of his close teammates over to his dorm room for a test of manhood. He'd pass around a bottle of whiskey he kept hidden in a cut-out section at the foot of his mattress and tell his impressionable friends to drink because today you've proven yourselves men.

Barry would drink twice as much as his teammates and still remain sober enough to celebrate at a bar in Ypsilanti. If no one accompanied him, Barry would talk to the bartender about life, football, the tension in Germany, Hitler, Europe, how easy it was to pass his classes, and his early high school victories when his father would give him a beer after the game and say, "Tonight, you've proven yourself a man." Barry would drink it down and his father would give him some more, until he heard the chanting of the crowds in the stadium: "GALENA, GALEEENA, GALEEEEEEENA."

* * *

I never care what people think about me anymore.

Sometimes I get up in the middle of the night and laugh out loud at all the people out there, at how stupid every single one of them is.

My father taught me too well. He said it was his moral responsibility to do so since my mother died in a car accident when I was twelve. Someone hit her. That is, she was walking on the side of the road, on the proper sidewalk when someone smashed right into her as she minded her own business at her peril. Didn't know her. I was raised with the wisdom of seldom being seen or heard by either parent—a nursemaid, and then several nannies did the day to day childrearing, each guardian unable to master the English language, hired from Dutch or Norwegian countries most of the time. I know my mother loved her long lost flapper prohibition days, drank gin like a beautiful fish. A long-forgotten wish was to get to know her, after she was gone for good, but my father remembered her as just a dame. Other women took her place quickly enough. Sad story. I know. My lost mother? Did I know her enough to love her? If my father didn't, I followed his lead.

I've got the upper hand now.

Everyone listens to me. Even if they did kick me off the team for drinking, they still think of me as a football star, one of the old-timers. Mary once asked me why I act the way I do. I told her I am at war. She thought I meant with her.

How could she possibly understand? She wasn't ever in Germany. Never stepped one foot in it. I told her to shape up. Eat less bratwurst and mustard.

She had Arlene eight months after I left Ann Arbor to join the army, after I finished basic training and was sent overseas, what everyone was doing. I mean, there I was learning how to fire a rifle, learning how to stop craving a beer every night, sweating in the bunk twitching into fevers, learning how to weave my way into enemy territory without being seen, and she's off having some kid she doesn't even tell me about until I get back. I never even wanted a kid and she knows it. When I returned two years later with no wounds and one lousy medal, she asked me what I was going to do. I shouted. I had forgotten what she even looked like, wanted to forget my past, and here she comes with a two-year-old messy girl straight up to my father's house. I drove her back home to Chelsea and told her to shut her screaming baby up and left her alone for a week. That's not my kid: I told her this as I turned my back. She called my father.

All he told me to do was marry her. I never wanted to marry anyone; I'm a field man. I wanted my freedom. The war taught me that. After I told my father I wouldn't marry Marion Spangler, he said that if I didn't he would cut me out of his will, a lot of money, a lot of power, a family hardware business now set to boom in rebuilding after the war—and boy did it grow, prosper, and make a killing throughout the next decade and on. As simple as that. I didn't expect this from him. We had learned how to be men together. All those nights after the games, all of the beer bottles empty and gone, and he laid this shit on me like I'm some daddy's boy who's never fired a rifle at a person before. I killed to come back to this. He said I shamed him too much, and it wasn't even the baby and the girl who now looked more frayed and out of control, weak, but still clinging the only way she knew how that shamed him; he said he'd never forgive me for throwing away the game. Football was the only thing that connected us. It's what we both missed terribly.

I asked him what was in it for me.

I remember him standing up so fast, but that is all before he punched me in the jaw hard enough to bring me to my knees, a real punch. That and more, he said to me. And then he threw his desk calendar at me and told me to pick one of the weekends in the next month for the wedding.

Arlene

Sparse light filtered its way under the bridge—just enough to keep track of those who wandered there out of the rain, sleet, snow, freeze. Topside, a cheerful contrast, strung along the bridge wires, holiday lights in green and red blinked. Crossing the span made most residents, even Arlene, nostalgic for Christmases from the past, stockings hung above roaring fires, Arizona holidays without snowfall or any discernable seasonal switch. The locals would point out every change, but that applied to every community. Only the two entrances, or exits, to the bridge were lit by the filtered streetlights mixed with the green and red. In the darkness beneath the bridge, Arlene wandered a separate distance from the few others, dressed in every piece of clothing in bulky layers; her feet scuffling over broken glass, hamburger cartons, and donut bags, tattered newspapers (yes, there was still a daily, and Arlene collected these papers to start fires with, only in secure barrels, to warm her hands), lipstick-stained cigarette butts. Not Arlene's; she smoked whenever she could scrounge up enough funds, but she hadn't worn lipstick in decades. The dusty red boots she wore had lost the lining months before.

As Arlene sat down with her back against a bridge support, she thought about how she had found the boots in front of someone's house, where the family brought out their trash once a week. She stared through the windows of the house as the family dressed and tinseled their Christmas tree, placed a white star on the top. She was wary of the young couple. They made her dream about her childhood.

In her vision she was young again. She saw Philby, who turned away from her in high school and left for college the next year. Her parents walked together for the last time when her mother packed up her station wagon and made sure the final papers were signed. Arlene stared out the window as the countryside passed, and she was young again and had met a courteous man who sat down next to her that first week in the dorm cafeteria. He'd ended up walking her to the undergraduate library. Keeping her gaze on the broken and cracked sidewalk leading up to the night book deposit box, he slipped his hand into hers. She pulled her hand away to drop the books in the slot. The two books were a week overdue, but she didn't care; knew the bill would be in the campus mail at some point in the future; knew she only wanted to grasp his hand again, quickly, and search for release. She made her own plans.

In front of that house a smile came easily to her, and a laugh was even easier to conjure up, so she laughed. The sound carried across the small college-house lawn, and the woman in the window pointed at her and spoke to the man who was her husband. The front door opened. When the storm door followed, Arlene turned away and whistled a tuneless melody.

She clutched the red boots to her chest and strolled towards downtown State Street where she could show off her find and ask people for cigarette money. The man on the lawn watched her go. He was going to ask her something about private property, something cruel would've come out of his lips, something he would've laughed about when he went back to his wife, but something about the small woman in the dirty beige coat made him keep silent. She did no harm, he would tell his wife; she only wanted those old boots of yours. Ann Arbor's holiday lights flickered as Arlene walked down Hill to State and watched the students filing into the Union, asked them if they could spare a quarter or a cigarette—'tis the season to give. When a couple of frat boys parted in front of her holding their noses and told her to take a bath, she turned and looked into the eyes of the tall one with the blunt haircut and said, "I was one of you once," and resumed her path. One of the kids looked nervous, as if he was worried he would share the same fate down the wretched line. The boys laughed and talked about the party this coming Saturday. Arlene stopped on the steps of Angel Hall, still, cracking, imposing stone columns rising up five stories, and thought about the camouflaged past her mother told, where she met her

father so long ago, and how, at first, they were so happy—
this part a fable. Arlene searched the trashcan for cans and
bottles to return, picked out a dented Diet Coke can, and
stuffed it into her large plastic bag. She left the steps of
Angel Hall and continued on her way to the lights of the
theater marquee on Liberty, where they were playing clas-
sic old holiday pictures, even a Bing Crosby crooner. Later,
when the morning chill came, she planned to go down to
the bridge and hide from the wind.

*　*　*

My life is full of chances now. Fate has nothing to do with
the way I choose to live. Even though I'm alone, I'm sure
there are still a lot of people, fewer in number, wondering
about the reasons why I do this or that—I don't stand
around simply to get hit by pity. When I'm lonely or out
of cigarettes and my check has long been cashed and spent,
I sometimes wonder myself. But I love my freedom. I go
where I want to go and sleep where I want to sleep. No one
can tell me what to do anymore. I hate my life. I despise
my past, the people in my past after my grandparents died
too long ago now to even remember what they looked like;
I don't have a photo of them stashed away in one of my
pockets. I hate myself and the man who came out of the
house with his fists clenched and I hate the way people look
at me and hate it that no one who looks at me gives me any
Christmas money and hate you and me and everybody and
hate and hate and hate.

　　Chances are I don't really hate myself. But sometimes
I love playing the part of the martyr because no one from
my old life would ever believe I choose to live my life this
way. I know they talk about it with my mother over coffee
in the employee lounge: How's your crazy daughter doing?
I saw her walking on South Division the other day. All the

nurses and doctors knew, everyone who passed me on the streets of Ann Arbor knew; they'd seen me on my vagabond journey, they looked down on me and my chosen homelessness—every street in this city was known to me. My father died a year ago and left me money, lots of it, I guess, from his business, stocks, bonds, and real estate, the old house I grew up in that has neighbors on all sides now and no more woods to explore, pits to fall down, development, development, but I don't care and I won't touch his money. A new lawyer taking care of my father's legacy tracked me down, gave me the formal papers, and I deigned to sign where they wanted me to sign, and then I turned my back on him and the past. The great Barry philanderer football star hid stunted dreams. Not one second of my life had been spent sympathizing with his troubles. I mean that. He remarried three more times, three younger wives, as he grew more decrepit and richer over the following decades. The divorces an escape, for these ex wives, from the same kind of verbal abuse, paying the exes little to nothing in the divorces, prenuptial agreements ironclad, created by his toady lawyer (who died five years before my father) who helped my father so much I wonder if they're in side-by-side graves.

My mother, who lives down Stadium, won't open her door to me anymore. Her young parents with different afflictions, Alzheimer's hit grandmother so young I didn't understand why she needed to be shuttered away. Even on Christmas day my mother won't welcome me. She thinks I'm a bad influence on Carrie, my little girl the state took from me when I took to the street. She's my one saving grace. I never want to see my Carrie influenced by the wrong type of person, and Lord knows what my mother tells her; I've always thought of my mother as the wrong type of person. Just because she thinks she cleaned up her life, got a nursing job in the emergency room, doesn't give her the right to take my child away. But then I forget that she's retired now, and hate myself for not remembering that simple fact. My child's grandmother shouldn't be the one looking after her. She should be enjoying her twilight years. I forgive her for getting a restraining order against me, and that she wants to raise Carrie because it's a second chance to get it right, something to atone for. I should know what's best for my daughter; I'm glad the father doesn't even know a thing about her, but my mother keeps her door locked and even has some type of seventh sense about her so she can tell I'm close. It gives her enough time to walk the other way as quickly as possible. That boy from school followed me around and we had fun, we graduated and moved in together for years, but I left him when he started hitting me. I can pick them as well as my mother, and the baby came and I didn't know what to do.

I don't even know how old Carrie is now. Is she a teenager? Impossible. She's much older now. Doesn't even live in the same state. Has she fallen down a long steep hill? What pit did my mother save her from? I can't help getting these facts wrong, what order they're in, what I choose to tell anyone who cares to listen.

My repenting mother and I raised Carrie together until my head burst. I went off. I can't explain it any better than this. I described a room filled with people, talking laughing living breathing people to my mother, to another doctor, and they turned, eyebrows raised in alarm (alarm for me), and said: "Arlene, there's no one there. You're all alone. Arlene, are you all right? You have the most peculiar thoughts."

All the old faces haunting me, an ache that turns purple, lines surfacing…my mind cracked, split wide open, too far to heal. For a short time I took medicine my mother begged one of her doctors to prescribe. Therapy with a University of Michigan psychological bigwig alongside my new drug-addled push for balance, again, my nurse, my mother, pulled strings to get me seen, and I soon turned into a drooling mess. These drugs made me feel like I'd been tossed into the deepest pit, that I floated in crushing bleak solitary fluid, dirty water, drifting there without being able to move up or down, and floating was supposed to be a wonderful sensation. P'shaw. At the soonest opportunity to escape, I felt compelled to go out on a walkabout, went missing, mapped Michigan's wilderness, and it was a good thing the weather turned early spring with balmy temperatures. I visited the lakes, the shore, watched sunsets and dawns up close and personal, quit the meds, and ran. I can take care of myself. Been doing it all my life.

Chances are I don't really hate my mother—can't speak ill of the dead, and my mother's been long gone, in some grave, a location unknown to me, and Carrie's up and flown away from me, from winter, from a past she understands nothing about. My child. Sometimes I look back at the way my mother hid behind some wall or some empty dream and can't help but think I have nothing but hate inside, for her—she spent her life, the early good years, taking and taking what my father gave her, all the good, all the bad, the apology jewelry, the Christmas gifts too ostentatious, too pricey, strings attached to every single one, she took all the I-love-you returns, plaintive and insistent, glorious trips to Paris, Bali, Texas, while her daughter was safe in Arizona, and she'd trade her life for one without all the pain and strict rules and yelling drinking stealing punching fighting pushing punching bruising screaming falling breaking boiling spilling cracking creeping smacking driving whipping and taking and taking what was given to her.

The End

SNOW GLOBE

SNOW FALLING. The low cloud cover formed a circular invisible wall. Shaking, I imagined someone—a giant, perhaps—shaking the globe and snowflakes falling, all of us shook up right along with them. That would be some party.

Enough snow fell to cover the tree branches, heavy enough to bow them down to the ground in graceful arcs, as if formally dressed for the party.

The Sawtooth Mountains and neighboring White Cloud Mountains held sway (on sunny days the ethereal majesty of the rugged landscape's raw nature brought tourists to silent contemplation—even in today's technological age), an extraordinary winter storm whiteout making them appear untouched over the past couple days. Here in Sun Valley, Idaho, the snowplows worked overtime to dig out people and their four-wheel-drive Subarus, Jeeps, and Range Rovers; some didn't receive service until the next evening.

"I love the weather we're having," the pale-skinned woman said to a man in black boots, jeans, vest over black-buttoned shirt.

"I prefer the snow to the negative degree temperatures we had all last week. I'm not cut out for this kind of freeze. Give me Palm Desert sun," said the faux cowboy in reply, as if asked his opinion. These two strangers at the first holiday party of the season just met each other, and their conversation became even more polite.

"I'm Rachel. I believe we met last year at the spring picnic on the mountain. Remember? All those bottles of champagne everyone brought up on the lift? They looked like soldiers in a row stuck in the snow banks next to the tables. So much fun! And Dean brought the best fried chicken." She extended her hand out, limply, egotistically, with Bette Davis brio.

The man in black shook her hand and said, "I'm Logan. How do you know Alex and Tobin?"

"Alex is my little brother."

"You've got to be kidding," Logan said. He chuckled a bit with easy, infectious humor.

"No—no, it's true. I'm the older, prettier sibling who tries to control his every move. And I'm not a lesbian either if that's your next question." Rachel let out her own laugh with a champagne-induced hiccup.

"I didn't even know Alex had a sister." Logan swayed, spilling a drop of his Ketel One martini with a twist of lemon.

"Well, then..." Rachel smiled with a questioning expression as if mystified by sloppy drunk gay cowboys. The diligent, supportive sister, she was there to spend the holiday with her brother, and she'd take the clumsiness of strangers for his sake.

"I think I need a refresher. Sorry if I spilled any on you," Logan said. He then turned towards the bar in the corner of the large two-story living area, a remarkable contemporary home on the fairway, close to an even larger house once owned by Arnold and Maria in better days.

"Merry Christmas," Rachel muttered under her breath.

The room, designed minimally in shades of white sand and gray, was decorated with ornaments hanging from the huge repurposed barn-beam rafters (painted white) by fishing line, and the effect was impressive—as if all of the colorful, antique ornaments of glass and tin floated above the crowd without visible suspension, on their own; jaunty, festive. A fifteen-foot Christmas tree centered itself on the far wall opposite the expanse of windows facing the ski mountain, Baldy. The tree had characteristics in common with the owners of the home: both immaculately dressed and whimsical; the tree was draped with only one kind of ornament, gilt and crystal snow globes, smaller ones at the top and larger ones circling the bottom. Everyone bois-terously exclaimed approval of the small, twinkling white lights showing the tree off. The special, most extraordinary snow globe was placed at the top of the huge tree, and this globe displayed its own Christmas tree with miniature snow globes alight, its own tree-topping snow globe encased there like a layer in an intricate nesting doll, rapturous. Instantly stunned by the tree, those arriving studied the details of all the snow globes of differing variety, displaying scenes from winters and cities around the world, and they gave props to the premiere party hosts.

Ted and I stood with Rachel until she departed in search of another cosmopolitan.

Alex and Tobin built the house six years previously when they wanted a second home, a ski chalet. They lived most of the time in another spectacular home in Santa Monica. Both were retired from the film industry. They loved skiing, and this winter they were determined to learn how to snow-board. Cooking good food was another shared interest; they enjoyed the peace and quiet of the canyon they lived down and the smallness of the mountain town. They didn't move to Sun Valley for the gay community; there was one, a burgeoning group, and in five years time they'd found quite a few men and women who felt the same way they did. They believed that being gay shouldn't be the most interesting thing about them. There were good gay people

and there were bad gay people, and so their life philosophy
blossomed and they met the rest of the valley's people who
just happened to be gay. Alex and Tobin felt that they were
somehow better off taking a sabbatical from the Hollywood
crowd, that they could escape to Sun Valley whenever the
atmosphere became too melodramatic, recharge from the
congested traffic. And it was Hollywood, the influence, the
social climbers, those people gay or straight, really, who
wanted something more; even if they were givers during
the holiday season, a few were takers—I watched out for
and hoped to avoid most takers. Alex and Tobin were part
of the cliques and dramas, sure, but they seldom admitted
this to themselves. I'd heard this before, this protestation,
from any number of people in attendance and thought
they were fooling themselves. This valley had more than
one prom queen. Alex and Tobin were no different. They
secretly loved holding court over the rest of the party
attendees, and tried so subtly to not show this quality.
Although they were sweet in nature, giving, witty even (not
snarky-witty either), there was a certain calculation to their
inquiries; who knew that keeping up with the gay-Jones
family could be so dull?

"Are you back for the winter?" asked Alex, coming up
from behind us.

"Yes, and it's so good to see you again," Ted replied. He
took a sip of red wine, one of the few braving this drink in
the mostly white room. Ted and I hadn't yet separated at
the party, but we would soon venture off on our own, to
meet back up and discuss the lives of others. We'd gossip
quietly in a corner, and then talk about driving home, spend
a moment figuring out who was sober, and I wouldn't take
another sip of my drink from that moment onward, I would
hold onto the glass like a crutch.

"Everyone thinks you two are moving to San Francisco
for good. Do you like your condo?"

"It's wonderful there, and yes, the condo's perfect for the two of us. Honestly, I'd like to move permanently, but Ted isn't so sure he wants to."

"Have you seen Tobin?"

"Not yet."

"Well. Merry Christmas to you. Enjoy the party. Try the spinach purses. They're delicious!" The small talk with one of the hosts finished. There were so many other air kisses to make. Host duties. Ted told me to have a good time, and to smile more, be welcoming, not my usual wallflower. Have fun. And then he also left, and I watched as he made his way over to speak to a group of people who may or may not be future clients of his. This town produced physical trainers like rabbits. A ski resort town filled with adrenaline junkies, and some of them were cute to observe.

It was a party like any other party. No serious talk; I deflected that. Nothing deep and involving. The thrill of being able to get married in Idaho still resonated as a subtext in the crowd, and I guess each guest there had to bring that up, but I resisted this talk, the inevitable question: When are you and Ted tying the knot? Truly unbelievable that Idaho, the reddest state in the country had opened its doors, flung wide open, to allow gay couples to marry. I hated the term gay marriage. It's simply marriage. There's no straight marriage. It's simply marriage.

The surface rippled with small talk and playful talk about who was snowboarding the next day, who was thinking of buying a new place in Portland. Alice and her partner Tracy, both, like Ted and I, unmarried, rumored to be moving to Palm Springs to get away from the cold—who's happy, who's not happy, who's remaining in touch with those who had left for good, and who could care less, the last said in an Oscar Wilde tone of voice, like a sitcom star who drops a line and then turns on her heels and leaves until the time is right for her to return and say something bitchy-funny to someone else.

I felt lost at the party. Eventually.

I sat on the most comfortable couch talking to someone I hadn't seen in two months and I plastered a generous smile on my face. I lived with Ted in a house we remodeled four years ago after the move to The West for the snowboarding—all the way from Michigan. I heard Ted mention my name and laughed inside. At a party, when someone asked me a question about my life, I tried to answer as if the question was asked of Ted; he tried to do the same thing in reverse. "I do miss San Francisco, and Ted misses the great weather, the restaurants."

"Do you think you'll end up moving there for good instead of splitting your time?" John asked, but I know he really couldn't care less and was being polite, being as natural as possible. He was one of those architect types who couldn't mask his negative thoughts well. You see: I was partnered up (may as well be married after all the years), but not dead yet, and John was single and OTM (On The Make, for anyone out there who doesn't speak single).

"I would right now. It was so hard to come back last week. Ted isn't so sure. He wants to try living in both places for a few more years—do a seasonal thing, winter and summer in Sun Valley, and spring and fall in San Francisco."

"At least you get to leave whenever you like."

"Have you tried the petite quiches yet?" I'm bored, and after nursing my one drink, I hope John doesn't think it's him I'm bored with; it's the whole scene. I changed the subject. I plead attention-deficit iPhone social media distraction disorder. Every other person in this beautiful living room leaves to go check his or her messages, emails, Facebook updates, share a photo of the tree, an up close shot of a favorite snow globe. It's today's party etiquette.

"They're really wonderful. I wonder who Alex and Tobin used for the catering? They know how to throw an incredible party."

"Yes, the party atmosphere is twinkling. Happy holidays to you." I excused myself and headed for the bartender, who quickly, efficiently, nicely filled a new glass with more chilled vodka and lemon. He wished me a Merry Christmas with too big a smile. Go figure.

Ted now spoke to an older man whose partner was flitting around the room in a white suit and a green and red-speckled bowtie. Too flamboyant for my taste, but it's a small town and you get all types and more, waiting to bust open that self-hating closet. The older man had recently recovered from a fall from one of his horses, which sprained his rotator cuff, and Ted was telling him what exercises worked to strengthen the muscles around the shoulder. Ted used to be a physical trainer, knew the name of every muscle, how to regain power after weakness. Ted also inherited a large sum after his father's passing, and he managed this asset through the massive economic seesawing. I liked that I had a job to fall back on.

I'm not as into fitness as Ted, but remaining healthy is a key component not to be ignored. I picked my sport: tennis, and it's a game anyone can play into their twilight years.

When in the valley I worked at one of the three bookstores in town. There were no chain stores, only independents, and in the age of ebooks and tablets, a town that can support several independent bookstores is my kind of town. Hemingway would've agreed with me. Maybe his ghost still haunts the land. You had to drive almost eighty miles to find the closest big-box bookstore, but few people did. The valley, with the fluctuating tourist industry, somehow managed to support all three stores. I worked as a clerk, and I only worked three shifts a week, enough for me. I loved the communication with those who also cherished books, reading. I worked every high season, winter and summer, and left to replenish energy in San Francisco spring and fall. Ted took up the slack for my seasonal unemployment,

studied to get certified to be a personal trainer, and was
hired in both cities we called home with the understanding
that he would leave and return, and I contributed anything
I could save. My boss hadn't minded because she didn't
have to pay me during the slow months, we called spring
and fall: slack, when the summer tourists left and when the
snow was melting and muddying the hillsides. She knew
how good I was at what I did, that I had a passion for sharing this love of, reading, good writing, and appreciated me
for the time being. I've always told her she's the boss of me.

There'd been problems with competition between the
bookstores. Please, one was a used bookstore that had decided
to try its hand at selling new books, which, naturally, worried
the other two bookstore owners. Even so, my boss didn't carry
a grudge when this happened. The valley was filled with
literary readers. Jealousy is a natural thing. Egos got hurt and
gossipy rumors flew quicker than the magpies; they owned
the air above the valley. Everyone who worked in bookstores
wanted to know what one bookstore did to another, who was
possibly going bankrupt but hiding this fact, who was trying
to get more free publicity out of the local weekly, who had
priority for the next library reading and signing event when
an author travelled to the mountain town, who was trying
to say bad things about the other store without being caught,
and it all swirled and dove into a waste of time.

Before working for my present boss, I worked for the
main competition up in the Sun Valley Mall, and had to
leave for personal reasons, not the least being the fact that,
at the time, the closeted owner didn't approve of my open
lifestyle (jealousy again), and I felt like I was being pushed
back in the closet each time I set foot there. I won't be made
to feel like a fool for being enthusiastic about books either,
selling them like a car salesman, which is what the owner
accused me of doing, so I left and never looked back. Now,
he's out of the closet, partnered up, happy once more, and

I was more than willing to bury the hatchet, let bygones be bygones. This ex boss of mine, and his new, handsome partner, looked happy together across the room marveling at the snow globes. Holding onto negative energy isn't my style. A good friend, a mentor in the business, once told me to not take anything personally, no matter how hurtful it may be. Discard ill news quickly.

The problem at the party was that all the owners of the three bookstores were also in attendance and I didn't want to be there with them, even though I was a lowly clerk and had no agenda. I loved my boss. She was (is) a terrific person, fair, funny, filled with self-deprecating humor—and her partner, Elayne, was (is) also a gem, and helped with the accounting. Plus, as I've said, and most bewildering, the other two competitive owners were also gay, and it's such a bother. Look at how we all can get along. Do your straight friends introduce you to their other gay friends just because they're gay? Who says all gays have to like each other? Usually, being gay is all two people have in common, plus a love of vodka with semi-polite conversation commencing.

I could only retain my pageant smile for so long.

A football game was on in the far bedroom and even though I couldn't tell you the difference between players and what each was supposed to do, I moved away from the snow globe room, away from the sullen bookstore owners, away from the competition, and sat down in front of the television. My glass was almost empty again.

There were other men in the room watching, a few women too, some of them lesbian, but half of them were straight and even more conspicuous, bent on mentioning, in some little way, that they were definitely straight. They said things like, "Man, I wonder if my wife's eating all the bacon-wrapped scallops. Those are her favorite things in the world. Have you met her? Do you know the score?" As if I'd played football in high school instead of having crushes on the quarterback and getting picked last for that rousing game of War Ball in gym class.

The gay men in the room could care less. It's great to be so threatening to another man's definition of masculinity. "I didn't think you guys liked watching football."

"This is football?"

Some people laughed and the straight man did too, in on the joke, and then he shouted like a sportscaster after his team did something cool with the football. Merry Christmas.

I hid in the straight room. Not from my partner—Ted was having a blast pretending to be enchanted by the appetizer spread and comparing catering horror stories—not from the other bookstore owners either; they could have all the fun dueling circles like cats across the room from each other, staking their claim. I just didn't have the energy. And that's when Gordon sat down next to me on the sofa.

"Can I speak to you?" My radar went up, and I wondered what I'd done now.

"Good to see you," I said. I held up my drink to clink glasses with his champagne flute.

"It's a nice party."

"That's what I hear."

"You and I haven't seen each other in a long time."

"Almost half a year. Mariel told me you had a theater job lined up in New York City. How wonderful, Gordon, really."

"I leave next month." I could feel my gut start to strain. Small talk with Gordon was beginning to form an edge.

"Congratulations once more," I said, "you deserve this terrific shot. I loved your performances here at the Next Stage Theater."

"I've been avoiding you. And Ted. All this time."

"That's too bad. I always wondered why."

"You think you're so great." Gordon slurred his words. At least he had lowered his voice. No one else in the room could tell he was throwing shade my way. I didn't change my party face. "I no longer wanted to be around anyone with money in this valley who thought I wasn't good enough to hang with."

"So it's a money thing? A class thing? You think I'm a snob. You don't want to hang with me or return my phone calls, texts, and I sent quite a few when I wanted to hang out like we used to do. And when I didn't hear from you, I thought you were busy with work and didn't think anything of your distance."

"I had to teach you a lesson. Remember around your birthday when you drove over to pick me up on your way back to your house for the party? Ted made dinner for the group."

"Of course."

"I gave you a CD of my favorite music."

"And I said thank you."

"But you didn't."

"If I didn't, I apologize, but I was hosting a party and time slipped away. How rude of me if I forgot to say thank you, but I'm sure I did."

"You didn't even play it at the party."

I was screaming inside. Can you hear me?

"Gordon. You accuse me of being a snob, arrogant, as if I was born with a silver spoon around my neck, and not the middle-class Michigan boy who traveled to Idaho not too long ago. Because of your hypocrisy, you've been withdrawn since my birthday. Six months have passed without communication between us. You came to sit in judgment of me. For not taking the time to make sure your feelings weren't hurt in some way?"

"I had to teach you a lesson."

"You've said that already," and my voice became gravelly, low, my tone short. I couldn't help it. I could see Ted glancing my way from the other room. He looked worried, as if I needed saving.

"You can't just play the little rich boy with me. I can't believe you could treat a friend so cavalierly."

"I appreciate you bringing this matter to my attention. I'm truly sorry you feel this way." The anger in my head came forth in a rush and I could picture myself throwing my glass into the fire.

"I'm saying this because I'm leaving and I wanted you to know the reason why I avoided you all year."

"What an utter waste of time. How petty we both are. Do you think you're the only one who feels broken? How adult of you to teach me a lesson."

I stood up and said, "Merry Christmas and good luck in New York."

"I was hoping to patch things up with you before I left."

"Certainly. You got it off your chest and I'm properly scolded. If you'd come to me the very next day after the party or a week after you gave me the music and told me your feelings were hurt at that time, this moment, this sensitive moment, could've been avoided. Let me speak as bluntly as you just did. I make friends with people who accept me for who I am, people who aren't worried about offending me and vice versa. You were teaching me a lesson. That's a lark. I didn't know I was still in school."

I left the room. Others did catch my last few words and they looked away. My fingers were clenched tightly into fists. I found Ted and told him we had to leave.

We said our goodbyes to the hosts and walked into the falling snow. I was shaking.

Ted led me to the car and asked what Gordon had said to me.

"He told me to have a Merry Christmas."

"How much have you had to drink?"

"Not enough."

The End

THE HERALDS

THE DOUBLE ESPRESSO TASTED like burning wire.

Another sip would do him in. His stomach vented perking, spiking pain, but Kenneth Herald kept this to himself. His complaints didn't necessarily fall on deaf ears. His wife, Carmel, tried her best to remain sunny. She's the one who made his espresso in the morning with organic beans from a country he had a hard time pronouncing. There was a time when coffee—*espresso*—became a primary concern, a near obsession.

She'd ask how his coffee was, how it went down, all the personal descriptions of functions, bodily, mental, spiritual, brought him to this point in the morning, two days before Christmas. The diagnosis had made her too interested in every facet of his operating system.

"Good as ever. The best." Another lie he threw on a growing mound of white, filthy, I-mean-well, "protecting you from the worst" half-truths. Why did he bother? Carmel.

"You don't look so hot. Want me to call the doctor?" The worry in Carmel's eyes became an almost-physical object he carried.

"Just stress and the new antibiotics. Can't wait till this bacteria is extinguished once and for all."

"Motivation, dear. It'll kill you as good as any bullet."

"I'll take Carmel's Motivational Bon Mots for one, please, Alex."

He finished his espresso all the same, burnt wire taste be damned.

"Did you take in the pants?" He asked this question with a softer edge, hoping to alleviate Carmel's worrying nature, which could turn into another pick-pick-pick session.

"The new seamstress at Mary Mary's did last week. I have to pick them up this morning. Another errand in the holiday madness. You and I don't have to be ready until four. The elves will set up the house and the workshop. Nothing for you to worry about this year."

"They always forget something—the reindeer bells, remember that year? Will that give you time to get there and back?" She had to drive to the mainland. Their island life was made simpler with bridges, and living in the San Juan Islands was a blessing. The simple life they'd always wanted in retirement. They'd read about the healthcare system, the hospital, long ago, and this is what made them settle there—ironic that it was the healthcare system that would eventually turn around and bite Kenneth hard.

"Haven't missed an event. That's all you need to concentrate on. I know you."

Kenneth let out an unfiltered sigh.

"How's your stomach today?"

"Same as it ever was. I won't be charitable, that's my fear, if that's what you're getting at."

Carmel walked over to her husband and pressed her hand on his shoulder. Silence. A small gift.

"You're the forgiving kind," Carmel said, "but we're both going to be late if we don't begin the day. Call the doctor. He'll have some answers, even two days before Christmas."

Carmel's husband harrumphed, stood, and left the kitchen. Shower, shave, change, loose clothes. He'd be changing into his red suit later on and didn't want to wear confining garments.

When he reentered the kitchen, Carmel was gone, her car backfiring and then sputtering out of their driveway off to her errands. Kenneth would have to remember to call the dealership to schedule an overdue yearly service appointment. They bought a Ford locally because they didn't have to leave Fidalgo Island, they could service it right here and then go play a round of golf while they waited...thinking about the year ahead. She worried too much, and not for herself first, something he'd wanted her to do for the longest time since the diagnosis four years ago.

The image of the G.I. flipped into his mind and he almost bit his tongue. The anger within couldn't be quelled. He hated the doctor, the doctor's insensitive nature, a complete stranger to him, someone he'd only been around for two hours, at the most, who felt bitter enough to ruin his outlook using a cavalier tone, as if bored with his job. This Doctor Newcomb was someone who had never learned to cultivate a generous spirit, a kind bedside manner.

Four years ago, at the Outpatient Clinic, in the Puget Hospital's new wing built with retiree fundraising dollars, he met the doctor for the first time, who, brisk and this short of snippy, said, "Mr. Herald, you followed all the instructions?"

Doctor Newcomb studied the chart in front of him, his eyes scanning the information, simple boilerplate details on what he should expect, most of which he kept to himself. He wouldn't make eye contact until he'd wasted another minute. The doctor's manners had been abandoned, and obvious to Kenneth, Doctor Newcomb was one of those less empathic types. At least let him be one of those who studied hard in school and wanted to be the best in his occupation. Someone Kenneth could relate to was too much to ask.

There wasn't even a 'Hello, I'm Doctor Newcomb. It's a simple procedure and I don't want you to feel any tension or need to worry. I'll place the scope down your throat. This should give us a picture of your stomach, check the esophagus, and so forth.' The doctor was on autopilot and going through the motions. Carmel stood beside him until they wheeled him away. They wouldn't see each other again until he came around, the anesthetic wearing off, groggy and feeling out of sorts, throat raw and voice hoarse as if barbwire had scraped the walls of his esophagus and stomach. It was shaping up to be a peach of a day.

Later, this same doctor, nonchalance a permanent shield, told them, with a removed tone, that he had Barrett's Esophagus.

"I see a lot of this. I'm going to get you a prescription—we'll check you again in a few years to see how this progresses, nothing to worry about at this point. Just start taking it and we'll check you again once your doctor approves of this treatment. Only thing to do now is wait and see how the new medicine works. Nothing to worry about." The doctor repeating himself made Kenneth even more suspicious and worried.

"What is Barrett's Esophagus?" Carmel asked this question and Doctor Newcomb acted like he didn't have time to become an encyclopedia, as if he was doing them a favor by telling them all about this illness.

"It usually shows up in people like your husband, people who've been having acid reflux problems, ulcers, stress-related problems. Are you suffering from any stress? Depression?"

"No," Kenneth lied, quickly, before his wife could respond. He'd be damned if he gave this doctor the satisfaction. What business was it of his what went on in his family's life? Stress? How about losing almost a third of their retirement? The financial worry made the acid in his stomach bubble.

The doctor handed the script to Carmel.

By the time they drove home, googled Barrett's Esophagus, and found out that too often, a significant amount of changed cells in the lower part of the esophagus become premalignant, and turn into esophageal adenocarcinoma (very much a deadly cancer), Carmel had shed her first tear. She wanted to know if the change in his cells could be somehow reversed.

What causes this condition is the continuous acid reflux, acid exposure, a condition increasing in our Western world, with 5-15% of people seeking medical care for heartburn finding out they are in for a wallop. The doctor's smug face, a prickly perfectionist, wouldn't leave his mind. He wanted to punch this horrid man.

He called his family doctor and told him the news.

"I'll get the report. Listen, this is very, very early stages, and a ton of people don't know they even have it and go on and live long and wonderful lives. Please don't add this to your worries. I'll call you back about the medicine. Once you begin taking that dosage other problems can occur."

"What's that?"

"I'd hate to see you on this medicine for the rest of your life if it isn't Barrett's. It's basically double your usual dosage of acid reflux medicine. It can also change what's natural in your system."

"A catch-22."

"I'm very sorry."

"At least one of you doctors hasn't forgotten how to relate to your patients."

That was four years ago.

Carmel worried so much about their dwindling savings that she took a job behind the desk at the Fidalgo Pool, checking in swimmers and aerobics class participants, and she was good at it, always smiling, sharing a laugh, and Carmel laughed easily—she had made real friends there: *The Girls*. Her new book group consisted of three other women from the pool whom she adored, Harriet, Mary Lou, and Callie.

They made her laugh and distracted her from worrying too much about her husband; she drew strength from their company, and hoped they knew how much she relied on them for easy wit, laughter, an uncomplicated camaraderie. Even so, Carmel didn't tell them everything. Her husband's health concerns were a secret that picked away at her sunny outlook. She was seen as an eternal optimist.

No one would know of her troubles, and her meager salary helped pay some of the house bills as their nest egg slowly recovered. In four years time, after scrimping on everything except their April vacations (which Kenneth insisted they keep on the schedule—"I'm not dead yet, he'd say, and we're not getting any younger!"), not going out except to walk the park or to listen to the free concerts at the marina in the summers, and they brought cheap wine and laughed with *The Girls* when they could join them. They cooked their meals at home, going out to restaurants only on celebratory occasions. Watched Netflix and turned off cable. Things were looking brighter. Their church had helped as well, singing in the choir—Carmel, not her husband, whose throat grew raw just thinking about what was growing there.

They decided to keep his diagnosis to themselves. Too many people would worry and proscribe and treat them differently. They treated themselves differently.

First, in his innermost secretive thoughts, a fear of mortality slivered into his very being, and this only made Kenneth more depressed. He was an optimist as well, almost as sunny as Carmel, walked on her side of the street. His glass was always full or mostly full or about to be filled. He knew that their obvious brand of optimism grated and made others roll their eyes, and even this made Kenneth and Carmel laugh and feel like they were the only couple in the world who felt like they did: Mr. and Mrs. Claus.

Carmel, although sunny and an optimist, had an intro-verted composure, and her husband had brought her out of

her insular shell. She complemented her husband's gregar-
ious nature, scolded him only good-naturedly. Seven years
ago, when Carmel retired after twenty-seven years as one
of the local high school guidance counselors, a friend from
church put an idea in her head. Her friend was reading from
the local paper, something about how one of the charitable
nonprofits helping disadvantaged children was looking
for a Santa Claus. Little did the nonprofit know they'd get
the both of them, a tinsel team they could be proud of to
this very day, a Mr. and Mrs. Claus who cared about the
children, listened to their wants—simple requests that dug
into their hearts, and made them laugh to tears back in their
home as they reminisced over the wondrous spirit gathered
around their town.

This help wanted ad stuck with Carmel, so much so that
by the time she returned home to her husband, she'd made
up her mind to recruit him as the town's best St. Nicholas.
Halfway there, he already looked the part. His extroverted
nature made him a natural. People even joked about him
being Santa Claus, and he did it for fun with all of his
nephews and nieces. Why not branch out? Share the spirit!

Carmel and Kenneth had no children of their own. No
grandchildren, and they decided long ago not to adopt even
though their siblings, closest friends, would always say they
should adopt. There were reasons why they chose not to
have kids, babies of their own. Over the decades, several of
their friends had babies and Carmel and Kenneth watched
as they grew up—but the reasons they chose to remain
childless had to do with their own upbringing, health concerns, and their love for each other. Some would say they'd
been selfish—couldn't understand love, how much sacri-
fice was necessary to place the needs of a child before one's
own needs, wants, loves. (They'd heard the parent's creed
so many times over the years: You're life is not complete
until you have a baby, a child of your very own!) Even their

own needs, wants, loves weren't the reason. Only Kenneth and Carmel's parents and her siblings knew, two brothers who were both geographically and emotionally distant from their sister—her parents passed away five years ago, months apart, after being married for close to fifty years. Kenneth admired them and Carmel wanted to emulate their easy bond, one filled with laughter, an intensely shared sense of humor. Kenneth knew that Carmel couldn't have children. It was physically impossible. Carmel's scare with genetics, carrying the marker for a horrible form of cancer, and undergoing surgery to ensure a long life, became a moment from her past that she would never forget, that made her grateful for not having a different life when she remembered her sadness, grief and her own losses. It was something she discussed with Kenneth up front...wasn't the first date, but another closely following that. "Listen, if you and I are growing closer, there's something I need to speak to you about..." And Kenneth listened.

Being Mr. and Mrs. Claus, they had so many children to look after.

*　*　*

They had both prayed for a miracle, spent too many sleepless nights tossing and turning. Truly, a veil would lift, a moment to think back on everything they chose to do after Kenneth's diagnosis. We get one life, Carmel thought, but she couldn't stop Kenneth from worrying himself into insomnia, a weight gain that although perfect for the Santa impersonation, wasn't healthy. She couldn't get Kenneth to stop worrying, and he wasn't worrying about himself first. He worried about her. A distant, but oh-so-close future she would have without him by her side. She winced just thinking of the rawness of his ulcer turning his cells into demonic ice picks. When at his lowest, Kenneth viewed his situation on an almost Biblical level, mentally punishing himself because he believed he had to atone for his sins although he couldn't imagine sinning so badly, taking the Lord's name in vein, thinking ill thoughts about his doctors, and finally, when Carmel became too anxious about her husband's depressed state, she sat him down and asked him what he really wanted.

"I'm worried about you. Being alone. People with Barrett's don't last five years once it turns to cancer."

"You don't have it, I feel it. You're just going on and on," Carmel said with a heavy tone of insistence.

"It's what I'm heading towards."

"You just had another check-up from a different doctor."

"And what will that show?"

Carmel didn't answer that question, but said, "At least he was more compassionate."

"Which takes me where again?"

"I'm going to call now to see if the doctor has the results."

They didn't want to go back to the same doctor. When their family physician asked why, they could barely hold back their criticism, and another doctor search commenced. They drove off island to a doctor's office in a crowded hospital block in Mount Vernon, a medical system surrounded by clinical doctors, dentists, opticians, and skin care service providers.

The new doctor, jolly, thin, willingly chatty with Carmel and Kenneth, told them he'd been a vegan for seven years, a vegetarian for the decade before that switch and he'd never felt better. Highly recommend it. They inferred that they probably weren't being as healthy as he was, but let that pass. Good for you.

"Hello," Carmel said, "I'm calling for the G.I. results for my husband. He's right here if you need to tell him instead of me. Certainly." Carmel handed the telephone to Kenneth.

He listened and his lips tightened. "Yes. I don't understand. Did my doctor say what to do now?"

More time passed. Kenneth listened and hung up as if stunned.

"What did he say?"

"I don't have Barrett's. Never did. They're sending the results back to our doctor now, but there was a misreading."

Carmel sat stunned as well.

"I can't believe it," Kenneth said, "What was that Newcomb thinking? He was probably too busy to get my diagnosis right." There was real anger in her husband's tone, and Carmel tried to wrap her head around what he was saying to her.

"It's wonderful news no matter how we got here." She moved over and wrapped her arm around her husband's shoulders. "Everything's going to be okay."

"I need to talk to my doctor and ask him about the medicine I've been taking for four years. He said that was just as toxic to the system. What a farce."

"I'll call him right now."

The turn, what Carmel would describe later to her friends at the pool as a miracle, changed Kenneth's mindset almost immediately—of course she swore Harriet, Mary Lou, and Callie to secrecy since she couldn't help revealing the too personal story now that it had turned positive. Of course they said mum's the word, and were elated for their friend, and Kenneth would understand. He was on cloud nine.

Darkness held on though in its tight grip, and the stress and ever-present worry transformed bit by bit into simmering anger at the initial misdiagnosis. If he ever bumped into Doctor Newcomb on the island he didn't know what he'd do.

"I'd like to punch him right in the face. Hard."

Carmel shook her head and said, "You'll do no such thing."

They spoke to their doctor and he had just received all the results from his second scoping, stomach, esophagus—a plan of attack, a new plan. No, he felt horrible about the Barrett's diagnosis, could only say that sometimes it does go away, but sugarcoating the blow. This was good news, and Kenneth, within, felt a blossoming lightness.

"So what about the medicine I've been taking to combat the Barrett's?"

"We'll help with that. There are ways to offset any damage that's been done, but that sometimes has further complications."

"I feel like a lab experiment gone wrong."

"There's one other concern. The reason you're feeling lousy recently, your stomach pain, is because of H. pylori; the biopsy results show you have this common stomach ailment, which causes 80% of all stomach ulcers. I don't know why this wasn't checked back then, but you need to go on a series of antibiotics over the next two weeks to get rid of it."

"And this is simple?" All Kenneth could think about was the incompetence of the doctors he'd dealt with. Why wouldn't his family physician catch any of this? Kenneth had to shake off his anger-inducing thoughts. If one more person told him he should do yoga and learn to meditate…

"It's common. I've treated many people with H. pylori. 20 to 40 percent of the population has some form of it and doesn't even know. It's a bacterium people get from food and water, but that's only a theory. Not much is known about exactly how people wind up with this stomach infection. I'm truly sorry about what has happened to you. We're going to get you better. On the right track."

Kenneth felt like he'd been given a pardon from an invisible warden. The madness had wormed its way softly into his thoughts, and he'd imagined a darkening skein of pain and finality. The initial diagnosis had pushed him to consider the most dreadful things. His dark, innermost thoughts would stay locked up tight. There was no way he'd share these with Carmel, with his drinking buddies on the island. The next Beer on the Pier event he'd buy everyone a round and he'd whoop and holler, like a kid. He could see himself getting drunk for the first time in decades, partying, celebrating. I'm not dying, Kenneth thought, and let out a held breath. Some fine day, but not today, and he was thankful.

He'd rewritten his will, streamlined it to make Carmel's grieving process simpler. That's what he had thought about. Washington was a state that allowed assisted suicide, and he wanted his doctor to know that if he became unable to live with the pain, he wanted that as an option. He'd gone down that road. Each year, in April, they travelled. He took Carmel to New Orleans where they ate the best gumbo on the planet, stayed in inexpensive hotels, splurged on a two-week cruise through the Caribbean—swung a two-for-one sale price, hiked as far up Mt. Rainier as possible on a guided tour. They didn't overspend. Their retirement savings, though lower than ever, would rebuild, and pensions would hold up; he wanted to experience good things while he still could. Live your life like you were dying. And he did.

* * *

"You've got the boxes of preserves?"

"Yes. Moved them to the back of the car this morning."

"We should be on our way," Carmel said.

"Kids wait for no Santa," Kenneth said.

"Patience? Kids? Ha! You look great."

"You too, Mrs. Claus."

"Mr. Claus, I do believe this is going to be the best Christmas."

"You're such a softy."

Mr. and Mrs. Claus drove to the outreach center. They carried box after box of miniature mason jars filled with Carmel's homemade strawberry and peach preserves, each jar lid wrapped in red and green ribbon. These would be given to the children after they told Santa what they really wanted. Even this early, the parking lot filled to capacity.

Cap Sante Marina had become the town's gathering spot and a group of carolers sang holiday classics a cappella off to one side of the community room. Men and women of the town, a ton from the local theater guild, FITE, the Fidalgo Island Theater Ensemble, dressed in fashion from a hundred years ago or more and sang with gusto; Charles Dickens would be proud, all that was needed was a Tiny Tim.

"Hello Santa!" A small child waved to them as he held his father's hand.

"Hello, young Sir!" And that was all it took to get Kenneth into the season. His shoulders straightened, his voice deepened for the occasional Ho Ho Ho, and he placed his red and white-fur-lined cap on his head.

Carmel made sure he was dressed to perfection, not a seam coming loose, belt shiny, boots clean. Beard trimmed. Check. Eyes twinkling.

They worked their way to the small area cordoned off where Santa's Workshop stood behind a North Pole sign, a few elves with pointy ears carried presents in and out of the small workshop. Kids formed a queue and watched the elves fill and tie up a large bag of presents. Another elf would take this bag and circle the building and unload the bag once more to begin again. The line moved forward. Parents pointed out Christmas trees, lights, the arrival of Santa and his rosy-cheeked wife, Mrs. Claus.

Kenneth walked over to a huge chair, which was throne-like with gilt-edged arms. Fake snow scattered on the ground. A festive air that made Carmel smile wider. She loved this moment the best. The first child she approached was probably five and holding hands with her mother.

"What's your name?" Carmel asked, bending down so that her curly, white bewigged head was close to the girl's.

"I'm Jennifer."

"It's an honor to be first to see Santa. Have you been thinking of what you want to ask him?"

The girl grew shy and wouldn't say another word. Her mother shrugged.

"It's been a long day. We've been standing here for so long."

Carmel let that go, in one ear and out the other. She'd heard all kinds of interesting things from the parents of the children.

"May I lead you to Santa? Here, take my other hand." Carmel patiently guided the young girl and her mother up to Santa's chair.

"Who do we have here?" Santa asked. "Welcome!"

"This young lady is named Jennifer."

"Go ahead, honey," the girl's mother said before lifting Jennifer up and placing her onto Santa's lap. "I can't wait to send her father a picture. He was called up two months ago for active duty. Jennifer, smile for your daddy!" The woman took a picture with her iPhone. "Tell Santa what you want for Christmas."

"I want daddy to come home." The nearby naval base repeated this pattern yearly.

There was a moment of silence. Mrs. Claus backed away and approached the next child in line, asked his name, and waited.

"Your daddy must be a brave man. Is there anything else you'd like? I'll work hard to make you happy on Christmas. Trust me." Kenneth worried about how sensitive children were, how his every word had mystical powers, changed a child's perception, and this child, the very first, had his thoughts spiraling.

"A puppy. Mom said I could have a puppy to play with." Kenneth glanced at the mother and she quickly shook her head no.

"Well. A puppy would be wonderful. Do you know that I don't have a family dog? I have too many reindeer to take care of."

"I want a puppy but I know I won't get one."

"What if Santa...what if I, surprised you Christmas morning. What if I thought about your wishes and came up with the best present that was made just for you and no one else. A present so different, so beautiful, that you'll share it with your mom and tell your dad about it the next time you speak to him. Can you think of such a present?"

"No."

"Well, I have something in mind. Mrs. Claus?"

"Yes...bring this little girl our first present. Do you like peaches or strawberries best?"

"Strawberries," little Jennifer said.

"Strawberries it is, then." Out of one of two large bags at Santa's feet, he pulled out a miniature jar of Strawberry jam, the green ribbon festive, and handed it to Jennifer. She took the jar with one tiny hand. Her mother grasped her free hand and prompted her child to say, "Wow! Thank you!" The next second she was pulled away.

"Here we have a young gentleman named Regis," Carmel brought another child up to Santa's chair, and his parents took photos as he was placed in Kenneth's lap.

"Oh, you've grown so much this past year, Regis. What would you love for Christmas?"

The hours flew by.

The kids smiled. Most left with jam. Their supply dwindled at the end, but even this couldn't stop the last gift-wishers from smiling. Santa and his wife worked well together. Those parents who insisted on receiving jam gave their addresses so that a small jar could be sent. Carmel was happy to oblige.

In the middle of the pack, Carmel saw Doctor Newcomb with a boy about six. She didn't even know he had a child, didn't even know if he was married or not since he didn't wear a wedding ring. She whispered in her husband's ear and his rosy-cheeked countenance tightened up for the briefest moment.

"Be Santa," Carmel said.

When the doctor's child sat in his lap, Kenneth said, "Have you been a good boy this year like your father?" He couldn't resist adding the last. Even this made Carmel squirm inside.

"Oh, yes, Santa, the best. I want a radio-controlled Maisto Rock Crawler Jr., the one that can climb everywhere and goes really fast but if you run out of that the Galaxy Morphibians Shark would be so awesome."

"Well, I'll check my list and see if I can really work miracles." Kenneth had never said anything remotely like that to a child before. The Doctor stood there with the dourest expression on his face. Who was he to judge him?

"Santa, I think it's time for your break. The elves have a question," Carmel said. She then helped remove the doctor's child from Santa's lap and grabbed her husband's hand.

In a moment, no jar of jam offered, the child and the doctor had vanished into the crowd. Carmel and Kenneth went into the elf factory and she gave him a long hug. Nothing more.

"Don't worry."

"Thank you for that. I told myself I didn't want him to affect me. Just seeing him made me want to smack him."

"He'll never know."

"And, you're right, now isn't the place or time to give him a piece of my mind."

"There are a few more kids. Buck up."

"One more minute."

"Come out when you're ready. I'll go entertain the last of them. Tell them they weren't good enough for my jam."

"Who is?"

Carmel laughed a laugh that only Kenneth would understand.

The End

BONUS CONTENT

Sandcastle and Other Stories: The Complete Edition will be published, with added content, by Booktrope. Two of the stories from *Sandcastle and Other Stories*, "Cats in Trees" and "On the Back Staircase," are set in my hometown of Granville, Ohio, at the old red farmhouse built in 1895. Those were fun years to be a child.

As a bonus, I'd like to share one of the more fantastical tales from *Sandcastle and Other Stories*. "Poseidon Eyes" is a rush, depending on point of view, of either sanity or delusion. Please follow Melanie Fortaine down another kind of rabbit hole, and decide for yourself.

Ever,

Justin

POSEIDON EYES

THE WATER IS A PART OF ME, a passion splintering my vision; it has always been a part of me. My name is Melanie Fortaine, and I live a life hidden by crashing waves along the California coast; it is where the dueling began. Everyone around me has changed so much and so often I appear to be unyielding and resolved; it's the choice I made. I'm a college senior now with one more summer season to drift by before I go back to my marine biology books, lecture paper, and honors thesis recording the influence of kelp beds on shark migration in the San Francisco Bay.

Last week I turned twenty-one and my parents set up the usual week-long stay at the Break Wave Hotel to celebrate—my mother always says she loves my summer birthday, and I deserve a lavish celebration. I know that's only partly the reason. The other part is her constant need to be seen as a kind of queen amongst her wealthy circle of friends, the party becoming more intricate with diverse themes and an increasing budget. In the current economy I told her a slice of my hometown pizza joint's to-die-for leek and potato pie would suffice, just the three of us, but Mother wouldn't hear of it. I gave in once more, but even so, I told them I'd be a day late, what with the drive down from Berkeley, where I was interning for a marine biology, green initiative, environment-driven corporation specializing in extracting toxins from any polluted body of water, and, yes, these companies do exist; we're not all in thrall to harsher corporate mind control. My mother sent their longtime driver to pick me up; they wanted to make sure I could still be trusted, to keep a watch on me; they thought I still had delusions even after all this time, water under the bridge. I haven't let it slip, not even once, that my delusions never went away. When your world changes you learn to adapt.

I make Jeremy stop at a branch of my bank. I have a check to cash, a present from my Aunt Evelyn. To me, when I enter the cold, marbleized interior of the bank, all the tellers look the same: I see them in three-piece suits, ties, dress suits the color of gray, brackish water; their skin is scaly and fishy, cheeks and jawbones encrusted with murky green barnacles. And they all seem to be staring at me with their fish eyes, blink-less, but maybe I'm just being paranoid because everyone always stares at me, as if I'm different, somehow mysterious. It's something I've adapted to; I now get a slight thrill out of it because it boosts my confidence, something I've worked hard to maintain since my low self-esteem became a daily dinner table conversation topic back home seated between Mother and Dad, their bulbous bodies shaking and negating all my distilled energy to bits. I still remember all the different therapists I was dragged to: flippers, gills, sharks, eels, and manta rays.

Since my vision was changed I see money differently. Pearls for large bills, speckled shells, coral for coins I keep in a small opening-eye purse. Whenever I have to cash a check, it takes the form of a clamshell that has to be scrutinized, examined to make sure it's good.

I move to the front teller and hold out a dull, old clamshell. It is large, covered with sea algae and the teller opens it as everyone gathers around. A pearl the size of a jumbo jawbreaker sits on a muscled, red tongue.

"We need two pieces of I.D. for this," says the teller. He grins like a tiger shark, suit stripes flamboyant smooth going down, and razor sharp if you run your hand against the grain.

"I don't have any."

Before I can open my mouth to tell him I always bank here when I'm in town, the man says, "This must not be your regular bank. When you get some, come back to me." I want to reach across the coral-topped counter and point out to him that my dad could buy this bank a hundred times, but that would be too much like my mother's haughty reaction, and I retreat, remembering humility and money and how it perverts.

The teller pushes the clamshell into my hands, and I watch as the pearl falls onto the cerulean area carpet. It rolls out the entrance of the bank and stops in front of my idling car. I can't figure out why the check bounced and then rolled and I begin to draw conclusions, flutters of the past, when strangeness flipped my world, when I had to become fluent in focusing on *his* presence, when I could tell *he* was in the same room with me, watching me, making the hair on my skin stand on end. I have a bad feeling forming in my mind. I realize no one else has noticed except Jeremy who steps out onto the sidewalk, picks up the pearl and hands it back to me.

"When was your birthday?" he asks in a voice mimicking cordiality and caring. I want to ask him to cut the charm out and tell me if he saw anyone weird watching me in the bank, but I know he reports anything strange I say to my parents, anything they can use to buckle me down.

I try to be nonchalant when I tell him, "I thought it was yesterday."

"Well, happy birthday to you anyway."

"Thank you, Jeremy. I'd like to go to the hotel now." We are all business now. He holds the door as I climb into the back seat of the green Jaguar XJ6, then he takes the driver's seat. The air from the open windows blows my blonde hair up behind me, and I let it obscure the back window. To my left is the ocean. The tide is coming in on the little inlet, and small children play chicken with the gently rolling waves. Jeremy watches the water as if mesmerized. Something odd is in the air. Hypnotic. Even though I know this is all illusion, I still leap over the seat to take the wheel because the car is veering closer to oncoming traffic while Jeremy gazes at the churning blue water. He turns to face me, but I'm not shocked or even surprised by his appearance because he has always appeared this way to me. His mouth is stuffed with black seaweed, forcing his jaw to drop, unhinge, and his eyes to bulge. Feeling a shiver of cold even in the hot sun, I sit back in my seat. I no longer care if the man drives safely or not.

Jeremy stops the car in front of the hotel. When he opens my door, I watch the seaweed glisten in the sun as it dribbles down his chin. I pick up my purse and hand him a small yellow-streaked pearl.

Seaweed falls from his mouth as he says, "You shouldn't have. Thank you, I mean. This is too much."

"That's all right, Jeremy. Just keep it. For old time's sake." I feel sorry for him and tell him to get a haircut. I then stroll over to the hotel entrance.

The door opens before I can touch it and I let a pair of walruses, the male horned and the female designer wrinkled, through the door first.

The male walrus tips his golfing hat to me. I wonder what they really look like beneath their masks and cover my mouth when I start to giggle.

I step into the hotel and pretend to be shocked when the lights brighten and a resounding chorus of *Happy Birthday* fills the room. My parents started this ocean-view family tradition back when I had my trouble, when I became so depressed that the mere sight of water, people, made me reach out for any sharp object, when I cut myself to rid me of the illusions. Now I thank God, the only true God, cuts heal over and leave me scars to remind me my life is not made up of interconnecting dreams. I try to put a surprised glint into my eyes and don't know if I succeed. Some of the longtime hotel workers I recognize wish me well and I smile back at them.

A bearded man in a black tuxedo thrusts a small rectangular box into my hands and fades quickly into the crowd surrounding me. Everything seems to be happening too fast, and I want to stop the man who gave me the gift because I realize too late that he looked human. Then I glance back at the crowd and blush. Trying to feel elated, trying to almost cry because they remembered my birthday, I say, "Thank you. Thank you so much." My parents bounce over and hug me as best they can. My mother never shows me much physical affection so I barely get an air kiss from the tip of her snout.

"Open it. Open it. Open it," someone begins chanting, making the others join in. The tone rises in volume and the chant soon turns to: "Open. Open. Open," as if all curiosity has lost itself and a commanding presence has taken over, forcing me to try to glance in all directions at once. I close my eyes to block out the leering faces. Then there is silence. Clamor too quickly cut off to be natural. I open my eyes. I remember games I played as a little girl, before I was tutored at home by Mrs. Shotplace, before Dr. Rutledge grilled normality into my head, before there were schools of fish children surrounding me on the playground, darting, where everyone moved when I closed my eyes, or when I turned my back to count down from fifty. Red Light Green Light, Mother May I, Hide and Seek.

The crowd has disappeared somehow. Only one person remains.

He is dressed in the same type of tuxedo as the other man, but his face is now shaven and he is a larger, more threatening figure. The man's voice is loud, booming through the empty hotel lobby the words: "Open it now."

I glance at the object in my hand. The box is now a large clamshell, and I'm feeling a dim vibration coming from within. The lip of the shell forms a taunting ragged smile.

"No." I feel the presence here and try to breathe normally, to not let him see my fear. I'm stronger now and even more determined to succeed. I'm not the same little girl who strolled his beaches.

"But you must. Can't you see, my angelfish, you must."

I bite my lip, drawing blood to dispel the images shooting into my head. With all my might I throw the clamshell at the beaming man. I've aimed for his smug, arrogant smile and…

*　*　*

When I was a young girl of seven, I yanked the plastic arms off my red-cheeked doll and filled them with sand. My mother watched me from a distance and told me I was going to break the doll, and didn't I like it? Dad gave that to you on your birthday, she said, dump out the sand and put the arms back on.

"No, Mom, I want to see how heavy she is when she's full." This was so exciting to me, the concept of weight, why my mother strove to keep hers down even when she was already skinny. I also played around with gravity and threw the doll in the air waiting to compare the "thunk" sound as it hit the ground: weighted and weightless.

My mother sighed. Reopening her novel, she started reading the same page she had just finished. Then she had to reread it again. Scowling, she threw the book down beside her and said, "I can't seem to concentrate today. I'm going back to the house. You come up when you're done playing." I knew she wanted to get back on the telephone with Mrs. Fairfax-Worthington to talk about their next doubles tennis match at the club, who they'd beat and who was opening their homes on the next house tour.

I said, "Okay," and fiddled with the doll's arms, trying to pop them back into place.

"And don't leave your toys down here." My mother turned, slipped into her sandals and stepped away.

"Mom?" I called out to her.

"What?"

"I'm going to collect seashells, but I won't go in the water." She worried about drowning deaths, the mothers she watched on Oprah discussing the loss of their children and how it ruined the family unit and caused more cases of divorce than any other reason. I wonder if my parents would get a divorce if I died, especially now that I'm older and willing to test the matter.

"Okay, sweetheart." Mother shuffled through the sand. It quickly rose into dune, heavily sloped, leveling off right before the stairs leading up the steeper bluff to the ocean-view house.

I watched her climb the stairs. I thought she looked beautiful up there. With the sun reflected behind her on the cliff side, I thought she looked like an angel, and I wanted to run to her and make her hold my hand and pay attention to me, tell me what it's like to grow up without a parent's touch, tell me she loved me more than anything else, more than new cars, tennis circles, drinking at the club, trips to L.A. and parties at the old, musty "stylish" hotel. "We do so much for you, Melanie. How can you say we don't love you?" And they'd try harder, all the while piling the material goods by my side to make up for lost affection.

The tide was turning. Barefoot, I dropped the doll parts and skipped down to the receding water, my feet digging into wet lip of beach. I wore a peach sundress and wouldn't have gone into the water even if she told me to. The dress matched the one my doll wore.

Even though I was only seven, I knew all about the animals living in the sea. Dad had given me a picture book encyclopedia full of sea creatures. I studied the wet impressions curving the sand, searching for movement. When a small dimple of sand started wiggling, curiosity made me thrust my fingers into the hole hoping to find a sand dollar, a crab or an octopus. Instead, I was pulled under. Something had hold of my wrist and yanked me down a dark hole that opened below. Unlike Alice I screamed and got a mouthful of sand.

*   *   *

When I was pulled under the beach I was too scared to think anything coherently.

My hand was jerked harder. Soon, I fell deeper and landed on the black-and-white marble floor of a large room. Air compression cushioned the fall but it hurt. In the distance, waves crashed against a wall-wide window, blue, green lighting playful and mixing colors and shapes, bubbles and life just beyond. Orange-striped fish swam right up to the glass, puckered their mouths, and gazed at the strange room under the beach. They stared at me. Fish can't blink but I wish they could. It's hard to sleep with your eyes open.

I spit sand out of my mouth and pinched sand out of my underpants. As I ran my hands along my legs, I thought: Mom will kill me when she sees how dirty my dress is.

I walked towards the window and the fish darted off leaving vapor trails of bubbles. In a second they were back, playing a game of petulance and happiness: who could scare whom first. The room was lit with some kind of blue light, softly glowing phosphorescence, but I couldn't tell where the light was coming from. I rubbed my bottom, which was bruised from the fall.

Appearing from nowhere, a man wearing a black tuxedo strolled onto the marble floor, coming closer to me. I backed away, trying to escape like the orange fish. He had a harsh face, with a hooked nose and large black eyes. The man said, "What are you thinking, my precious?"

I continued my retreat until I was pressed up against the glass wall, cold and humid-wet. In the air, on my arms, a warm mist drifted. This is a trick, I thought, a scary one. I'd been told never to talk to strangers, but somehow I felt compelled to speak to him.

"Who are you?"

Rising from the floor, a desk appeared. After he pointed at the ground again, two chairs also clicked into place. The desk and chairs were polished pink, yellow, and peach coral.

"Have a seat, pretty lady."

I had heard the word lady before, and couldn't think why this man would want to call me that, but I sat down anyway, gently so as not to hurt my bruises.

"Now—what is your name, my dear?"

"Melanie."

"Do you know who I am, Melanie?"

"No." I wanted to go back, climb the stairs to my house, look like an angel way up high, and sit with my mother, make her hang up the telephone and listen to my story, put my doll back together and rip its head off. I wondered what it would be like to be made of sand. I would be heavier, I thought.

"I come from your history. I live in the water at all time— all at once. I have many names." The man seemed puzzled, his brow lifting, because I was staring away in the direction of the crashing waves. "How are you feeling?"

I fidgeted in my chair, dug my fingernails into the coral armrests. My face betrayed my boredom. I didn't like the man, and was still scared of him, even though he talked nicely to me, but I was never interested when my parents asked me basic question after question about how I felt or what I did that day because I knew they really didn't care too much; they'd say, "That's nice, dear. Would you please watch television or go play with the Green girls." I wasn't interested now that another adult was asking me questions. I thought the water splashing against the window, throwing the fish, was much more exciting so I concentrated on that instead.

"Do you know who I am? Stop picking at my furniture." The man's voice grew louder and the waves roared in response. I stared at the man once more and wouldn't budge again if he could do all that; I kept my jaw firmly shut. I wanted to tear his arm off and fill him with sand, prop him in a corner on my doll shelf.

"Is something wrong, my little starfish?"

I shook my head no. But there was.

"Well, let me begin. I've been keeping an eye on you, my sea rose, for some time now. Ever since you started skipping across my beaches, and I must say you are one of the most exquisite, innocent, delightful mortals I have seen. I want you to stay with me, by my side. You'll grow up under water with every wish fulfilled. And when you're older, you will rule all that you see." He pointed out the window and the scene changed to a land not glimpsed by many: the ocean floor lit up for me to see, but it wasn't one part of it, the vision showed all of it at once, magnified and drawn back with what I wanted to see. It was like sitting on top of a mountain, the highest peak in the world, and being able to see the land, the enormity of it, laid out before you like a quilt of green and brown, gray cities and dust. Under the water, the colors muted and whisked my breath away.

Countless ships, wrecked by storms past decades, littered the floor. All the creatures flew and darted like birds, the water becoming air and the coral the trees they flicked in, between the branches, shadow and light.

I didn't care much for what the man was saying, really I couldn't understand what he was trying to say, but I knew what the word stay meant and I yelled out, "NO." The glass wall became opaque, closet black.

The man plucked a clamshell from an inside tuxedo coat pocket like a magician and offered it to me. I felt my arm moving, and the clam placing itself gently on my palm. I watched my body move of its own accord and grew even more amazed and scared by the power I couldn't ever comprehend.

"Keep this then, fair creature of the air, as a token of my affection. One of these days you'll join me of your own free will."

"What? I want to go home."

"You will be mine because I was told you were unobtainable, unfathomable. The creatures of the sea tell me we will dance duels until the end, you and I, but I won't force you to stay because I cannot do so without your consent; even gods have rules they must abide by and games to play, but open my gift carefully. It will change your entire perspective." Then the man laughed without moving his lips, water roaring in a torrent. Only for an instant could I see how he really was, his true physicality, how his tailfin swished the floor behind him and the scales glistening on his forehead. Then I saw black tuxedo approaching and I began to shiver more when I started to levitate.

*   *   *

Another strange man, someone walking along the waterline at the same time I was trying to dig my way out, was offering me a hand. He helped me out of the sand hole and watched

as I ducked my head and raced off in the direction of the
private beach's restroom shack. I didn't know what to say
to the man who had just helped me; he was someone else I
didn't know, someone I couldn't trust. Almost in a state of
shock, I kept telling myself I had a nightmare on the beach
and everything now was fine. But I held the shell, the gift, in
my small hand. I searched for my mother in the sand before
remembering she had gone home long ago. The sun was a
sliver against the ocean, crimson when it dropped below
the horizon and lit the sky, diminishing with every second.
The stranger who had pulled me out of the sand hole wiped
his forehead and continued his stroll. He was probably
watching the beach for signs of more buried children.

When I was inside the restroom, I unbuttoned the front
pocket of my dress, put the clamshell in it, thought: perhaps
I should just throw it away, but then curiosity broke and I
quickly took it out. I stared at the lip of the seashell so hard
I thought it would open on its own. But it didn't. My fingers
pried and scraped at the edges and I kept thinking about
how my body wasn't mine, how I still had no control over
what I was doing.

I opened the shell slowly, only letting it crack the slight-
est bit, but that was all that was needed. A bright blue light
shot out and pierced my vision, a blurry ache formed in my
head. Then the light died. Rubbing my eyes with my fists,
I wondered what I'd done. Then I opened the shell all the
way and found a pearl split in half lying on the red muscle
of the clam. There was a thin strip of paper under the pearl.

The paper was yellowed with age and felt whispery to the
touch. At that time, I could only understand the first few words
written on the paper: *Now you have Poseidon Eyes*. The strip of
paper disintegrated before my strangely tingling vision.

When I returned home to my parents' oceanside villa,
my mother was a bottle-nosed dolphin and my father was
a humpbacked whale.

*   *   *

My mother asked me where I had been all this time. It was almost dark out and she was about to call the police when I walked in covered with sand, the fine granules another layer of skin on my body. I knew that she wouldn't expend energy looking to see if I was safe. The brusque quality in her voice was as close as she got to caring that day.

"How did you get so dirty? What were you doing, Melanie?"

"I was under the sand." I stared at my mother and started to hiccup. "You're a dolphin, Mom. You've changed." I spoke slowly. Her eyes, small and flat, yet sparkling with unnatural glee, opened wide.

She ran her flippers along my scalp checking for bumps. "Did you fall and hit your head? Is that why you're talking nonsense?"

What I saw my mother do to me was a bit different. They were flippers brushing at my hair. It even felt different. My father came into the kitchen. I saw his hands first because they were the same as always: large, tanning-bed even on the palms, and hairy between the knuckles. The head and spine of my father had been expanded, extended, and replaced with the features of a whale. I wondered about my parents, how could two different species mate and make any child, someone like me?

I covered my eyes with my hands, screamed a high-pitched, dreadful scream and ran to my bedroom. My parents stared at each other, and my father asked my mother what all that was about.

*   *   *

I watched the psychiatrist read from his notebook. It was my first visit to this doctor's office and I didn't like it at all. After a few weeks my parents told me I would get better, have fun even, if I went to the doctor, and no, I wouldn't have to worry about needles, shots.

I was still only seven when my parents decided to stop my craziness by hiring the best child therapist on the west coast. I thought about turning eight in another month. Of course, my parents would take me to the hotel to celebrate, as they did every birthday. Farther down the shoreline. Next to the ocean. They only sent me to the psychiatrist because all their friends sent their kids. I heard Mrs. Fairfax-Worthington, while drinking with my mother, her Bloody Mary Buddy, say that, "She'll grow out of her problem. She just needs to talk to another adult who won't criticize her. Someone she can tell her innermost secrets to." And then my mother said, "I guess so," and then, "Melanie, stop twiddling around please. Go get the tennis ball I hit over the fence." And the shame of my "problem" was known by anyone my mother came into contact with. In school my friends shied away from me, and I heard whispers about how loony I was. As I grew older, more kids came around me and told me it was no big deal seeing a psychologist; most of their parents did too.

My eyes had dark rings around them, suffocating the deep blue irises I was often complimented for. I closed my eyes because, in the way I saw him, Dr. Rutledge had the pudgy body of an adult male in his mid-forties but the face of a large bulbous, yet sleek-nosed electric eel. His long neck snaked out of his sport jacket and sparks jumped onto the floor, sizzling the bargain-priced oriental carpet, something inoffensive to match the cookie-cutter landscapes-of-light paintings hanging from the office walls.

I had found the last month and a half almost unbearable. Somehow my vision had changed and an eel with a sharp row of spiky teeth was calling me young lady just like the man who lived under the sand. I instinctively disliked Dr. Rutledge and found myself clamping my eyes shut so that I wouldn't have to look at him.

"Melanie, would you open your eyes for me?"

I did and found the doctor gazing as understandingly as any other electric eel would. I closed my eyes again so tightly shut lines appeared on the sides of my face.

*　*　*

When I returned home after my session my mother wanted to know what happened. A spray of water burst from her air hole as she talked in her squeak-squeak tongue.

"Nothing," I said.

"Come back here, missy. I'm not paying good money for you to tell me *nothing*. What did the doctor say to you?"

"He told me to open my eyes and stop fooling everybody."

"Well. I think that's good advice."

"But I'm not fooling anybody. He's an eel, Mom. I can show you his picture in my animal encyclopedia. And you're a dolphin. You even eat more sardines and order extra anchovies on the pizza. I only like cheese." I started to cry. "And Dad is a whale, and there's a man under the sand who did this to me, and he said he's watching me everywhere I go."

"Stop it, Melanie. I don't want to hear you when you talk crazy like this. You're only going through some phase like those talk shows say all children go through; maybe you're too old for your age. You're just not eating enough or sleeping enough. They say eating more fish helps, the oil does something, your doctor even said so, but you don't like fish. Seaweed also. It's supposed to be good for you."

I stopped crying and stared at my mother's row of tiny teeth. Since I saw my mother as a dolphin, she was always smiling, always had a stupid look-at-me grin on her face. Sometimes I even heard my mother squeal like a dolphin, high and ear-piercing when she found a new piece of sapphire jewelry downtown or when she watched the Tonight

Show and woke me up with her shattering laughter. My mother was talking underwater gibberish.

"Can I go to my room now?"

"Okay. But you think about what Dr. Rutledge said. And try to get some sleep. We'll eat dinner later than usual. We're going to Andante's for lobster tails."

*   *   *

In a year's time, one session a week hadn't helped me. My parents didn't know what to do with me. I started cutting the underside of my wrists, letting the cuts heal and scar before making another incision. I couldn't go through with it though; I didn't have the courage. No one noticed except the maid who washed the dirty red towels, and she was too timid to say anything to my mother. The maid appeared to me as a kind of camouflage fish, blended into the background wallpaper in splendid fashion, and she also wouldn't say anything because she couldn't speak English very well and she didn't have her green card yet. My parents stopped making appointments with Dr. Rutledge.

In school, my teachers thought I was disruptive and destructive. I earned some respect from the rednecks and the other cut-ups, but the rest snubbed me, but always came back to me anyway because they knew my parents had lots of money and they thought my stories about what I saw were funny. My art teacher was especially upset with me when I drew a picture of a lamprey: jawless, its mouth circled with sucking, rasping teeth and wrote the art teacher's name underneath it.

When I turned twelve, my parents decided to hire a tutor to teach me at home. Mrs. Shotplace handed me an English grammar book and taught me how to spot adverbs and map a sentence. In my eyes, Mrs. Shotplace had the face of a puffer fish. She would swallow air, expanding her body enormously, whenever I said something wrong. I decided lying about the things I was seeing was the only way to cope.

Depression overwhelmed me on my thirteenth birthday when my hormones started to change. The creatures around me thought I'd put the worst behind. Everything wasn't the same; I had lived within this undersea world for so long now I was taken for granted, and I was found to be strange and little more than a curiosity; I became withdrawn and had no real confidante to help me through the hard times, like when I was watching a movie and couldn't relate to the two seahorses shooting bullets at the blowfish who wanted to take over the town. Mrs. Shotplace wouldn't be back the next year. My parents were starting me in a new junior high school, very private and selective, and they told me all the time how they had to "grease" a few palms to get "their" schizo kid into the place so I'd better not mess everything up. My mother was now becoming like me for some reason, and I think it was the years of emotional trauma my visions had put her and her pride through. She was quieter now and rarely spoke even when spoken to.

A week before school started, I took one last look at my mother, the dolphin, and my father, Mr. Moby, and told them I was going down to the beach for a swim. There wasn't a response, only a lifting of the flipper and a short sigh.

The undertow pulled me under and I welcomed it and remembered the sensation of falling; this time I wanted everything to end peacefully as I jerked with the motion like a pulled puppet attached to an invisible string. But then I was coughing up salt water and gazing into the first human face, real nose, eyes, mouth, lips, cheeks that I'd seen in six years. He was a young lifeguard with shiny black hair melding the forehead. He told me I'd have to be more careful when I swam off the beach he protected, smiled at me and even helped me home after I rested for a bit under a red-and-white striped beach umbrella. I never saw him again, the beautiful human lifeguard, but from that moment on my life took a new direction.

My parents noticed the change right away. I was smiling and happy and talking to them constantly now, letting them in on everything I did, but not talking to them like they were fish or mother's friends were incapable of eating anything but mud grubs like the carps they were. Mother took this as a sign of how wonderful the therapist sessions and the private tutoring she planned had really been. She took me on a trip to New York City where the Statue of Liberty became a swordfish caught in the folds of a net, and I wondered how telling that really was. She even let me give her a kiss on the cheek before I went to sleep; one night a year later, she even said she loved me and wouldn't think of trading me in for anyone else in the whole world. I wondered how many times before, when I had fish-mouth, she wanted to do just that. My father blubbered and doted on me as if I were seven again, untwisted, before the change. To him I was still his little girl and he wanted to make me happy. I didn't think they really understood me, but I loved their new personality change as much as my own.

I studied harder in school and even made friends with some girls in my math class. We complained about the story problems and the boys who wanted to start dating us even though they looked like they hadn't even developed yet. My breasts were growing, and Mom bought me my first real-size bra. My math friends started inviting me to sleepovers and they didn't even think strange thoughts about me like the kids did in my other school. I saw them as outgoing tropically-vibrant fish. My parents relaxed during my fifteenth year and thought they had finally gotten through to me, had put the past to rest.

I graduated from high school in the top of my class when I was seventeen. I was voted most likely to succeed and everyone considered me to be the most independent person in the school.

I wanted to be an oceanographer, to work with the sea and the prizes within. In college I made these plans.

* * *

It's as if I never threw the shell. One second my arm is moving, the clam shell grinning, spinning as it plows through the air towards the man in the tuxedo, and the next second I'm standing in the same position, close to the hotel entrance doors, gazing into the man's coral eyes, thinking about throwing the clam shell at him.

"If you throw that shell at me again, you'll regret it."

"But I did," I say.

* * *

"Do you want to give up now, my little lost manta ray?"

I turn my back on the man and close my eyes. I start to count down from ten.

"I won't be gone when you're done with your numbers. I came to wish you a happy birthday."

I try to keep reign on my emotions, evenly, in control. There is so much I want to say. It's been so long since I was seven, so long since our meeting under the sand that I think of it as a dream, that everything around me is the way it's supposed to be. That I have nothing to fear; he said he played by the rules because there were consequences unmentionable if he didn't. That's what I believe anyway as I open my lips to say, "I can't believe you'd ever come back here." The mantra repeats, evenly, without a hitch, no stutter, I want to be in control. "I used to wonder why you did this to me. I began to believe everyone was like me, saw the same way I did. I tried to forget about you and what you did so long ago. Now I don't even care at all." I ignore the man, keep my back straight as I move, wander over to one of the lavender flower-print hotel chairs and seat myself gently onto the cushion.

"You're very sophisticated now, for your age, my dear." I cover my eyes, so I can't see the man hovering in the air above me. I forgot he could levitate and the sensation runs back to me, the feeling of sand gritting down my skin and suffocating, clawing at the beach. "How old are you now? Nineteen? Twenty? It doesn't matter. You're grown now, ready to accept my responsibilities. I'll still want you when you're old and no one wants to take care of you or even see you. I'll still be here for you. If you come with me, you'll remain young, immortal forever by my side. It is arranged by the gods—who know how fickle humans can be. The pieces are in check and they're watching me now. Don't disappoint me, my precious manatee, for I hate to lose." The man pauses while a beard grows instantly from his face. "I can look any way you want me to, change to suit your fantasy." The beard disappears and his hair color changes to blond and his cheekbones soften. His fingers roll curls into his new hair.

I can't help watching; it's fascinating, but the hardness in my stomach returns and I balance my gaze on the floor. Suddenly, inside, I am boiling with anger. I want to say, "Well you can't play with me. You can't just treat me like a trophy to put on a shelf to talk about to the rest of your kind," but I didn't because I think he'll leave faster if I don't pay any attention to him. I have adjusted myself to my life and vowed long ago never to have anything to do with the man if he ever reappeared.

"Remember, my sea sprite, the time you turned thirteen? You were so forlorn." His brow is sweating and I can sense the tremble of angst. Or what I would call fear. It's in his manner, predictable. He's pulling out all the stops now. The stakes must be tremendously high in his game. The light in the room dims and a wall lights up in the distance like a movie screen. I can hear the sound of waves crashing. Then a picture forms across the wall and I watch as a younger Melanie, a teenager again, runs along blinding white beach searching for her own mystic entrance to the water. She dances with the edge of the surf and finally wades in up to her waist. Letting the waves bob her gently back and forth, she coasts along the shore almost out of reach from the undertow. Thinking: come and get me—try to find me, in and out, in and out, bobbing along, belly hovering with surf, rising with the crest, gliding effortlessly, the bubbles dipping and ladling her out farther, passing the line of undertow. Saying: catch me by the ankles and pull me down deep where I won't have to watch anymore, see the world through my Poseidon eyes. She swims out farther with the waves calling her back as they pass in the opposite direction: you must not, you break our rhythm, you will find nothing, pleading with whitecaps, speeding towards the beach to ricochet and journey back with her. The scene changes to show sunrays breaking clouds in the distance.

I glance at the man and understand. He is there, in the movie; about to make his grand entrance.

"Make it stop," I tell the man. He only chuckles and shakes his head no. In my mind, I scold myself for showing him a reaction.

On the film, the younger me, I, slips below the waterline, her arms limply following her body down, flinching. A lifeguard appears out of nowhere, breaking through the waves with precise strokes from his muscular arms.

"That's me, my little sea anemone. You're so pretty and I've come to save you."

Hugging Melanie to his chest, the lifeguard with the shiny black hair sidestrokes to shore where a crowd gathers.

"It's the first time you let me kiss you."

The lifeguard tells the people to move back and then performs mouth-to-mouth resuscitation on Melanie.

"I should've known it was you," I say.

Melanie coughs salt water out through her nose and mouth.

"You were the only one not changed. I saw you as human, while everyone else there had grouper heads or something. Why didn't you tell me then?"

Letting Melanie lean on his shoulder, the lifeguard walks her into the shade of a red-and-white beach umbrella.

"'Be careful,' I said, 'I'm always watching.' Not a big enough clue for you, but enough to play games, and that's what I like to do. Besides, you were still too young, and anyway, I saved your life didn't I? That deserves something." The anger is building within.

The nerve of him. He thinks so little of human life. How can you win against someone like that?

The movie vanishes and the hotel lobby lights come on. A school of rainbow trout waddles up to the check-in desk. I wonder if the man really sees them the way I do. The sea snake behind the counter presses a buzzer and a bellboy with sharkskin appears. He piles luggage onto a cart and motions for the school to follow him into the far elevator.

My thoughts coalesce. In front of me for the first time in years is the grinning man, god, chess player, whoever, who has tried to create my world; play games with me; control me from a distance. Finally. Take it to the limit and leave. The resolve, my independence, I'd built up within myself over the past eight years since my near drowning has forced a confrontation and I won't buckle in.

"You think you can show up whenever you like. Disrupt my life with your special effects." I stand up and point my finger at the man's face. "Well I'll let you in on something. I didn't know much when I was little, but I've learned to live with myself. I don't care about what you did to me anymore. I have real friends and great parents even if they do look like they live in your watery world. Do you hear me? I couldn't care less if I spend the rest of my life surrounded by fins and gills. I've had plenty of time to get used to it thanks to you, and believe me, I do thank you. If not for your little lifesaving stunt, I never would've learned to appreciate my life and the people in it. If there's anyone else betting against you who's watching us right now, collect your winnings because this game's over and he's lost."

The man's amusement turns to silent fury. I can almost see his true features once again, like a ghost image, the tail-fin flies behind him and is controlled once more, disappears. His eyes widen and he grinds his teeth together. For years he has waited until I was old enough to reason with, and now I've become too defiant, a creature of impossible-to-harness petulance. In his gaze I can tell he craves me even more, and my heart tightens like it did the first time he called me his pretty lady.

"And another thing, Mr. My Little Fish Shit, I've never been happier than I am right now. I wouldn't even want you to change my vision back. I don't even think you could." I'm running on pure bravado now, and I stop talking so I can catch my breath before giving this away, until I feel my heart stop racing. He wants me because I was made an object in a war by some higher power, nothing more, but I can also feel his longing, and I really wonder if a god so cruel can ever know what the word love means.

"You say these words without thinking. I ask you once more, and I'll keep asking you again and again until your stubborn phase is broken. Come with me."

It's more a demand than a civil question, but I answer quickly enough and turn my back on him. Then I say, "Go away."

I take a deep breath and head for the hotel stairs to go look for my parents.

"Excuse me, Miss?" I hear the words and watch the shark-skinned bellboy approach. I think he's kind of handsome; the tough skin gives him a rugged look.

"Yes?" I say.

"A man told me you left this in the lobby where you were sitting. Is it yours?"

In his palm sits a large clamshell. It is white, almost pure, polished to an unnatural perfection.

The End

ACKNOWLEDGMENTS

A new book, a new adventure, doesn't simply materialize out of thin air, even Christmas tales filled with the magic and wonder of the season need a lot of wizardry.

I thank Rachel Thompson for the coolest introduction to Booktrope and for being a good friend through life's ups and downs. All writers, all people, live a series of highs and lows, and after the past few years, I have tried to find a balance I can be grateful for and share with others.

Thank you Katherine Sears for taking my books into the Booktrope universe. It's so kind and generous of you. The writing life is an enthusiastic one, and I am a bit driven by this obsession. The Booktrope team I am in cahoots with doesn't hold that against me—ha! On that note, I must confess that I adore Stephanie Konat. Her timely guidance, the planning and coordination skills of a thoughtful Project and Book Manager, is greatly appreciated. It's like finding a lost twin, and I know all about twins. I also want to thank Shari Ryan for designing the coolest book cover for Hark—A Christmas Collection. I cannot wait to see what Shari's creative mind thinks up next. Jessica Reyes has a keen eye and her editing skills are topnotch. She helped to guide the prose, fix what needed clarity, and is a wonderful asset: thank you very much.

AUTHOR PAGE

Justin Bog's first two books, *Sandcastle and Other Stories,* and *The Conversationalist*, will be published in Complete Editions by Booktrope—please look for these suspense tales with expanded content. Justin Bog's *Sandcastle and Other Stories* was a Finalist for the Ohioana Book Award 2014, as well as being named Best of 2013 Suspense Anthology by *Suspense Magazine*.

Justin Bog (pen name for Gregory Justin Bogdanovitch) was born in Allentown, Pennsylvania. He is a twin, and his parents, both artists, travelled to several different locations looking for work that incorporated their artistic passions. They settled in Granville, Ohio, where Justin and his siblings were raised. Justin left to attend the University of Michigan, where he concentrated on English and Creative Writing. Afterwards, Justin received an MFA in Fiction from Bowling Green State University and then moved to northern Michigan. That was a short two-year sojourn, which ended when Justin moved to Sun Valley, Idaho. In each of these locations, Justin worked in independent bookstores and loved talking about books and authors with other readers. From Sun Valley, Justin moved to Fidalgo Island part of the San Juan Islands north of Seattle. He's now married to his longtime partner of over 26 years and they both look after their two long coat German shepherds, Zippy & Kipling, and their two barn cats, Ajax The Gray & Eartha Kitt'n (she has a secret she wants to tell you).

You can find Justin by email and he encourages your communication. Please let him know what you thought of his first holiday story collection. Or search throughout Social Media to sign up, follow, and Like Justin's Author Page on Facebook.

If Hark—A Christmas Collection hits with inspiration, please take the time to write a review at Goodreads or the online retailer of your choice. This helps authors so much.

Email: justinbog@mac.com
Justin Bog A Writer's Life Blog: www.justinbog.com
Facebook Author Page: https://www.facebook.com/
JustinBog1
Twitter: https://twitter.com/JustinBog or
Follow @JustinBog

Address: 1004 Commercial Ave., #480 Anacortes, WA 98221

MORE GREAT READS
FROM BOOKTROPE

Outside the Spotlight by **Sophie Weeks** (Fiction) In a world created by human ingenuity and dreams, Isabella has lived in Christmas for over four hundred years. But when she seeks a vacation and visits the foreign genre of Mystery, she discovers that the world of ideas is more dangerous than it seems. If an idea is murdered, does it bleed?

Pacific Sun and Other Stories by **Cris Markos** (Short Stories) Pacific Sun and Other Stories explores the extremes of the human experience: from genocide and human trafficking to poverty and terminal illness. From Bosnia to Kentucky, these stories inflect the best and worst of the human psyche.

Spots Blind by **Linda Lavid** (Short Stories) Stories about being blindsided—sometimes by family, friends, and lovers; sometimes by our own refusal to see the truth.

Summer of Government Cheese by **Paula Marie Coomer** (Short Stories) A collection of darkly introspective short stories. As they say, one way to dispel darkness is to expose it to light.

Discover more books and learn about our
new approach to publishing at **www.booktrope.com**.